The Elephant Girl

Elephant Girl

JAMES PATTERSON & ELLEN BANDA-AAKU

with SOPHIA KREVOY

JIMMY PATTERSON BOOKS
LITTLE, BROWN AND COMPANY
New York Boston London

JIMMY Patterson Books / Little, Brown and Company
Hachette Book Group
1290 Avenue of the Americas, New York, NY 10104
JamesPatterson.com

First Edition: July 2022

JIMMY Patterson Books is an imprint of Little, Brown and Company, a division of Hachette Book Group, Inc. The Little, Brown name and logo are trademarks of Hachette Book Group, Inc. The JIMMY Patterson Books® name and logo are trademarks of JBP Business, LLC.

The publisher is not responsible for websites (or their content) that are not owned by the publisher.

Library of Congress Cataloging-in-Publication Data
Names: Patterson, James, 1947– author. | Banda-Aaku, Ellen, author. | Krevoy, Sophia, author.
Title: The elephant girl / James Patterson & Ellen Banda-Aaku with Sophia Krevoy.
Description: First edition. | New York : Jimmy Patterson Books, Little, Brown and Company, 2022. | Audience: Ages 10–14 | Audience: Grades 7–9 | Summary: "James Patterson and award-winning Zambian writer Ellen Banda-Aaku deliver an unforgettable survival story of a Maasai girl who faces down poachers to find a future among the elephants. Clever, sensitive Jama likes elephants better than people. While her classmates gossip—especially about the new boy, Leku—Jama takes refuge at the watering hole outside her village. There the twelve-year-old Maasai girl befriends a baby elephant she names Mbegu, Swahili for seed. When Mbegu's mother, frightened by poachers, stampedes, Jama and Mgebu are blamed for two deaths-one elephant and one human. Now Leku, whose mysterious and imposing father is head ranger at the conservancy, may be their only lifeline. Loosely inspired by true events, *The Elephant Girl* is a moving exploration of the bonds between creatures and the power of belonging"— Provided by publisher.
Identifiers: LCCN 2022021791 (print) | LCCN 2022021792 (ebook) | ISBN 9780316316927 (hardcover) | ISBN 9780316317030 (ebook)
Subjects: LCSH: Maasai (African people)—Juvenile fiction. | Elephants—Juvenile fiction. | Poaching—Juvenile fiction. | CYAC: Maasai (African people)—Fiction. | Elephants—Fiction. | Poaching—Fiction.
Classification: LCC PZ7.P27653 Elc 2022 (print) | LCC PZ7.P27653 (ebook) | DDC [E]—dc23
LC record available at https://lccn.loc.gov/2022021791
LC ebook record available at https://lccn.loc.gov/2022021792

ISBNs: 978-0-316-31692-7 (hardcover), 978-0-316-31703-0 (ebook)

Printed in the United States of America

LSC-C

Printing 1, 2022

To Saada and Kweku, thank you always and forever!

—E. B-A.

*To my dad for encouraging me to embark on every adventure
and to live life to the fullest, and to my mom and my sisters
for their unending love and support.*

—S. K.

The
Elephant
Girl

PROLOGUE

My personal hiding spot was just fifteen steps from the watering hole. The water was light brown, and the edges were sloped and muddy from the paws and hooves of a thousand animals. Buffalo, monkeys, zebras, gazelles, lions. On one side, there was a fallen tree with dry, dead branches surrounded by green brush. On the other side were spiny bushes with round, dark fruit. Acacia trees surrounded the watering hole.

It was a quiet place—but dangerous. Which is why I kept it a secret. Whatever worry I felt was outweighed by my need to make a haven of my own, away from the village and all its rules. As a twelve-year-old girl, I was willing to take risks for my privacy. That is part of the magic of youth—being happiest in a place where no one else thinks you should be.

On that special day, I hadn't seen any animals, just a flock of silly sandgrouse wading at the edge of the water. But later that afternoon, I looked up again and there they were. Elephants. *My* elephants! It was the herd I'd seen before.

I was always amazed that animals so huge could move with such grace and ease, as gentle as the wind. As the elephants approached, I ducked back deeper into the brush and watched. The female I called Shaba was in the lead.

I saw her lift her trunk like a flag, sniffing the air. *Can she smell me?* I wondered.

If she could, she didn't seem to mind. Shaba led the herd to the edge of the water, and they began to drink.

My heart was thumping so hard I was afraid they might hear it. No matter how many times I saw the elephants, I always felt a power that went straight through my chest.

Shaba turned away from the watering hole, and I

could see what looked like a pink stub sticking out of her backside.

Is she hurt? Is she sick?

Her gray cheeks puffed in and out, and her big ears flapped. The other females crowded around her, but she backed away.

I could tell that she wanted room.

As they shuffled back and forth, the elephants kicked up swirls of reddish dust, and for a few seconds I couldn't see what was happening.

After a minute or two, Shaba stopped and spread her back legs wide, like she was about to sit down on an invisible stool. She shook her massive head. Suddenly a shiny wet sac spilled out of her and dropped to the ground. Inside the sac, the shape was clear.

I couldn't believe my eyes. A baby elephant!

ONE

I felt Momma's eyes on me the whole time I was getting dressed. She had that glassy look she did sometimes when two feelings were fighting within her, as if she were trying to make up her mind whether she was happy or sad.

It had been that way ever since Baba died. I could always tell when she was missing him, like right now. Even though almost four years had passed, whenever I thought about Baba too much, I felt a stone in my throat that made it hard to swallow.

"You look beautiful, Jama," Momma said to me, both of us looking at my reflection in the small glass mirror leaning against a wooden table. She was lying in the way that mothers do.

I do not believe I am beautiful, maybe not even pretty, though it might be said I was something like "cute" on my best days. Normally, I much preferred the comfort of my school uniform, but that day I got a thrill from dressing up for a special occasion.

I did like the new shuka Momma's friend Busara Kandenge brought back from her last trip to the markets in Nairobi. Momma had taken one of the carefully folded cloths—large square pieces of fabric in the traditional plaid pattern our people, the Maasai, had worn for generations—and draped it over my slim shoulders, tying it at the waist just so, to make a dress.

Then she fastened around my neck the necklace of large bright beads she had spent weeks making. We Maasai were known for our beadwork and our elaborate necklaces and jewelry. The necklace Momma made for me was a flat circle of ten rows of red, blue, and yellow beads that formed a wide, colorful collar. Today everyone would be decked out in all their favorite pieces.

I fingered the polished beads made of bone and clay and smoothed the soft wool of my shuka. The bright yellow-and-red plaid was flattering against my dark skin, and the necklace made me feel elegant and grown up—just like Momma.

Momma handed me some blush and a container of coconut oil. Makeup? This was pushing it a little much.

"Momma, do I have to?" I hated the whiny edge in my voice, but I also didn't want her to take this primping thing too far.

"Oh, come on…just a little. It won't hurt." She began to massage the coconut oil onto my shaven scalp until it shone.

I could tell she was enjoying herself because she hummed the tune of "Malaika," an old Swahili love song. *"Malaika, nakupenda Malaika,"* Baba used to sing to her. *Angel, I love you, angel.*

While she kept singing about a man who wanted to marry his "angel" but didn't have enough money, I allowed her to rub small dots of the red crème onto my face. As a last touch, she fastened a yellow-beaded headband across my forehead and tightened the tie of my shuka so that it would stay in place no matter how much I danced today.

"There," she said to me, satisfied, her eyes glassy again.

TWO

Being beautiful was never something I cared much about, but I was pleased when I looked in the mirror one more time. My eyes, which normally I don't like because they are too big, today somehow looked like they fit better with the other parts of my face. And the blush highlighted my high cheekbones, which my best friend, Nadira, called my best feature. I was happy with how much at the moment I looked like Momma, who was genuinely gorgeous. Everyone thought so—especially Baba, who always said that she looked like a woman you wrote love songs about.

"Today is going to be a wonderful day, Jama."

I nodded with genuine enthusiasm. I had been looking forward to the Eunoto ceremony all week, all month, maybe even my whole life, actually. This was my first. Even though our village had become more diverse over the years, we still held traditional Maasai ceremonies for the Maasai members of the community.

I imagined all the boys, the junior warriors, who were also preparing right at that moment for their big day. Everyone from our village would gather to watch them officially become men, ready to marry.

In ancient tradition, the boys would live together for ten years in the emanyatta, a warriors' camp, where they would learn how to survive in the bush and to prove they were strong and fearless by completing tasks like killing a lion. The training would prepare them to protect the tribe's vast herds of cattle, our pride and strength as Maasai.

Our warriors were long feared, as they conquered other tribes while moving around looking for grazing land. But periods of disease and drought killed many of our people and cattle. On top of that, the white people arrived and stole land from the Maasai. Even the fiercest warriors with the mightiest spears were no match for invading armies with guns.

So our traditions have had to change. Now the men had to go to school and work, and they didn't have the time to spend ten years in a warrior camp. And even without the new laws that have made killing wild animals illegal, no one would even think of killing a lion unless there was no other choice to protect our herds.

I thank Enkai up in the skies that the animals are protected.

THREE

'll go see if Kokoo Naserian is ready to go," I announced to Momma and bounded out the door and across the short distance from our enkajijik to Baba's great-aunt Kokoo Naserian's.

Our manyatta is smaller than that of some other families, just four enkajijik Momma built by hand with help from her friends, layering mud, sticks, and grass to make each small round room and roof. She then built a boma around all four huts, a fence so thick with sharp vines that no wild animals would think of trying to get in.

Our hut was small but cozy, and Momma and I

slept close together, side by side on grass mats on the floor, so that I could fall asleep or wake up to her soft snores. There was a small window covered by a mesh screen, and through it I could watch the sun rise, the birds fly by, or the rain fall.

I passed the two other huts before getting to Kokoo Naserian's on the far end. A thin stream of smoke rose from the enkajijik we use for cooking, right next to ours. Next to that the thick smell of leather greeted me from the one Momma used for her sandal-making business. Those two enkajijik were actually supposed to be for all the many, many children Momma and Baba had planned to have (one for the boys and one for the girls), but that didn't work out. They were only able to have one child—me—before Baba died. So it was just Momma and me and Kokoo Naserian.

A few chickens pecked and clucked at me as I passed through the yard, and our skinny goat eyed me lazily. My job was to milk her, and I would need to do that tomorrow, and also collect eggs, but for now I stayed far away so as not to get dirt on my new shuka.

I leaned into the dim, narrow doorway of Kokoo Naserian's hut. At school we had electricity, thanks to a large, loud generator, but at home we didn't. Kokoo

Naserian was just fine with that because she didn't trust it. Her opinion was that natural light comes only from fire and sun.

Despite the bright sun hanging in the sky, I could only see her eyes, cloudy and yellowing, in the dark room lit by only a small candle. I held my breath against the musty smell—like karanga stew left on the fire too long—but not so that she would notice. Momma would murder me if I showed any disrespect to anyone, especially our elders.

Kokoo Naserian was so old she said that if Enkai up in heaven didn't recall her back to the soil soon, the teeth that had fallen out of her mouth would start growing all over again. The other villagers had little patience for her long-winded stories, which she peppered with endless proverbs, but I adored her.

"Supa kokoo!" I greeted her.

"Supa. Is that you, Jama?" she asked, squinting into the halo of light streaming in behind me. Kokoo Naserian was also more than a little bit blind.

"Yes, Kokoo Naserian. I am here to get you. Are you ready for the celebration?" I walked over to her small wooden chair, made by Baba, to give her a kiss and help lift her up. She felt as light and delicate as a hummingbird in my arms.

"Yes, child, I'm ready. This will probably be the last Eunoto before Enkai calls me back."

"Don't say that, Auntie."

I was used to this. Every day since I'd been alive, Kokoo Naserian announced that death was on her heels, even though every day she lived on, stubborn as ever and ready with another story and another lesson, and a pocketful of cashews that she munched on all day long. It was impossible to believe she wouldn't live forever.

I didn't know Kokoo Naserian's exact age because she was born before people wrote birth dates down. She told me they measured age by the seasons. A child who lived through three rainy seasons was three years old. I guess the seasons were pretty regular and reliable back then because global warming hadn't arrived to mess up the environment and the weather.

Kokoo Naserian was born about ten seasons after the British forced the Maasai from their land. From my history lessons I know that happened in the year 1911, which made her around one hundred years old.

This was why she had so many tales to tell. I was fully prepared for her to start in with stories of Eunotos past and give me a long lecture about the importance of maintaining our traditions because Kokoo Naserian's favorite subject was "the old ways," but that morning she was uncharacteristically quiet.

FOUR

Kokoo Naserian leaned heavily on her walking stick as we shuffled slowly to the thatched gate of our boma, where Momma was waiting for us.

The sun glinted off the sparkling beads that formed a crown around Momma's shaved head. Her bright smile took up the entire bottom half of her face. For now, happiness was winning over sadness. Momma always said that we would be okay if we could keep that balance right.

"Are you ready to dance, Kokoo Naserian?" Momma called out, a gleeful sparkle in her eye.

The old woman attempted to swing her neck from side to side, laughing.

When we got close to Momma, I suddenly threw my arms around her in a big hug. She looked just as shocked as I was that I had done that.

I wasn't a little girl anymore, always hugging Momma or climbing into her lap or tugging her hand, but in that moment, I had this feeling that I was a child again, as if Momma were walking me to my first day of school.

Sometimes this happened lately, a feeling that came out of nowhere. Sometimes it was joy, or just as often it was anger, mostly that Baba died. These feelings washed over me without reason or explanation, like rainstorms.

I felt shy as soon as I let go. I walked a few steps ahead the rest of the way.

We followed the rocky dirt path past our neighbors' manyattas, which were already empty since everyone had left for the ceremony. We passed many cattle pens, some of the cows' big eyes looking up from the grass to follow us as we walked by. I loved that the land was so flat and that I could see far in the distance in all directions, endless stretches of tall tan grass dotted with dark green bushes and acacia trees.

When Kokoo Naserian was a little girl, our people still moved around a lot over many hundreds of miles, allowing the vast herds of prized cattle to graze in different pastures, but now we've settled into towns. It would be nice to travel around and live in different places in different seasons, but it is also nice to have a home.

I was born right where I live, in the same room where I still slept every night. It was all I'd ever known, and it made me feel safe to know this land, its smell, its sounds, like I knew my own body.

Just then two goaway birds, with tall crowns of feathers like a unicorn horn, swooped down and let out their distinctive loud call, like the squawks of a newborn baby. They called to each other again and again as if they knew there was a big celebration today and shared our excitement.

Kokoo Naserian moved so slowly that it took twice as long to walk into the village as it normally took for Momma and me, but soon we started to smell the roasting meat and hear the horns and the general commotion of excitement getting louder and louder. It sounded like all of Kenya had come to celebrate.

FIVE

Everyone was gathered in front of the school, a small one-room building made of red bricks bleached orange by the bright sun. Across from the school was a row of small stalls, tables separated by corrugated metal sheets, where people sold fruit and beads and grains.

I left Momma and Kokoo Naserian there and went to find Nadira. I was hoping she would be with her family, but she was gathered with a group of girls from school—Halisi, Endana, Lisha, and Kitwana—in front of the big silver bell at the edge of the schoolyard.

They made a tight circle, shoulder to shoulder, as

intimidating and impenetrable as the tightly entwined fence of our boma. Just like a lion, I would have a hard time getting in, so I started to turn away, but Nadira had already spotted me and waved me over, shuffling a little to make room for me.

"Is that my Jama, in makeup? It *is* a special day!" She laughed teasingly and put her palm to my cheek. Then she grabbed my hand and squeezed, and I was so grateful.

These days, I never knew which Nadira I was going to get. Sometimes it was still like old times. We had, after all, been playing together side by side since we took our very first steps. Our mothers said we were sisters born under the same moon, just four days apart.

Nadira knew every secret that I ever had in my life: how sometimes I felt that it was my fault that Baba died; how I once stole a small stone bracelet from our mothers' friend Akini's market stall just to see if I could, but then returned it because the guilt ate away at me; how I was so scared when my blood came a few months ago because I thought I had cut myself down there and would get an infection like the one that killed Baba.

Nadira always understood and didn't judge me.

For her part, she told me secrets, too, like that sometimes she didn't believe in Enkai but that she worried he would punish her for not having faith in him. I laughed and explained that she couldn't both worry what Enkai thought of her and also not believe in his existence. She laughed then, too. I was relieved to realize that although she questioned her belief in Enkai, it persisted nonetheless.

Lately all her confessions were about Jehlani and how she dreamt about him and how badly she wanted to be allowed to marry him and how she couldn't wait to move to Nairobi one day and go to places where she could dance with Jehlani to loud music.

I might like to go to Nairobi one day, too—minus the dancing to loud music. But as for Jehlani, I didn't understand why she, or anyone, would want to marry him. Or any of the boys we knew, for that matter. All they wanted to do was play soccer and make sure everyone was looking at them.

This was part of the problem with Nadira and me. All she wanted to talk about was boys and getting married and what a great wife she was going to be, even though she was only twelve like me. I had started to realize that while she and the other girls dreamt about being *with* them, I dreamt of having the same freedom and power as the boys. Then I could run as fast as I wanted, and learn as much as I wanted, and also hate skirts and dresses without anyone judging me and reminding me what was "appropriate." I could maybe go to university even, which is what I longed to do. I wanted to study ways to help the animals and the earth, which was becoming too hot and dry.

Standing with the girls, I felt my cheeks grow hot remembering how a few weeks ago, after school in the courtyard, Nadira had told me that some of them were talking about me. "Jama's head is up in the clouds," they had said. "She thinks she's so smart."

I don't think Nadira meant it to sound as mean as it did. And, anyway, they were right: I did believe I was smart, and I didn't think it was a bad thing, either. But that is how they meant it, so tears had still pricked my eyes. I blinked them away so quickly that Nadira wouldn't have noticed.

She had been distracted anyway, staring at the boys playfully wrestling in the schoolyard. Just like she was staring now. All the girls were. Their high-pitched giggles sounded loud and unnatural. I looked over to see who they were watching.

SIX

Leku.

The new boy had been the source of much attention and gossip since he and his family moved here a few months ago. Leku stood with his father, Solo Mungu, an imposing man, tall as a giraffe, who was wearing the dark sunglasses he never seemed to be without and his camouflage Kenya Wildlife Service uniform. As the new head ranger responsible for patrolling the Naibunga Conservancy, he was supposed to help stop poaching there.

Just a few weeks ago, representatives from the conservancy came to our school. With its reserve of land that bordered our town and a staff that was mostly Maasai, the conservancy was unlike the KWS or other organizations that looked after the safety and survival of wildlife in our area. The staff explained all about poachers—men who roamed our land to kill elephants and take their tusks and sell them in China, where ivory was in great demand. They shared many sad statistics, such as that twenty thousand elephants were killed across Africa every year.

I did the math—that was around fifty-five elephants *each day*. At the rate elephants were being killed there could soon be none left in the world. The death of any creature brought me sadness, but when it was a death at the hands of heartless, greedy poachers—a death for nothing—it made my blood boil. So I was glad that Solo Mungu was here to crack down on the evil poachers once and for all.

If they could be stopped with a look, then surely Solo Mungu would be successful, because he was a terrifying man. His mouth was fixed in a grim line, angry and serious, completely at odds with the happy celebrations raging around him.

His son looked angry, too, but that's how Leku always looked, like he'd chewed bitter herbs. He'd only been at school since the start of the term, but he'd already gotten into at least four fights with the other boys. It seemed like he was trying to prove something, though I didn't know what.

I didn't get what his appeal was to the girls. Not only was he as aggressive as a hippo, but with his big square-shaped head and short stocky legs, he looked like one, too. And as usual, they were going on and on about him. I wondered if it was just because they were tired of all the boys we grew up with and he was new and shiny.

When I looked up, Leku was staring right at me.

"He's looking at you," Lisha gasped.

"You should wave," Nadira whispered, laughing and elbowing me in the side.

Before I could even decide if that was something I would do, someone shouted, "Look—the warriors are coming!"

SEVEN

The crowd parted swiftly and made way for the breathtaking sight: a dazzling parade of dozens of men carrying large spears and wearing red shukas to symbolize war and blood. Their hair was dyed red with ochre, too. Their mothers had applied the color at the start of the ceremony.

Next to the school was a giant old baobab tree, as ancient as the earth itself, with a trunk as wide as a car, and that's where our spiritual leader, Laibon Umoja, sat stoically. He was almost as old as Kokoo Naserian and had the longest arms and legs in the world, which made him look like a spider.

We all watched and cheered as, one by one, each warrior approached him and touched his shoulder with their own to demonstrate respect. Then the warriors danced the Adumu, bouncing up and down, and chanting their gratitude for Enkai and prayers for mercy. Holding their spears, they took turns leaping into the air, competing to see who could jump the highest. The higher they jumped, the more we all cheered.

When I looked over again, Leku and his dad were gone.

Nadira and the girls had turned their attentions to Jehlani, who was at the front of the pack of warriors, wearing an elaborate headdress that didn't move no matter how high he jumped. His face was marked with an intricate pattern of red paint. He was the handsomest boy in our class—even I could appreciate that.

It wasn't just the girls looking at him; the boys did, too, everyone captivated by his line of perfect white teeth and taut muscles rippling as he jumped the highest and yelled the loudest. Like the others, his hair was in long dreadlocks down his back, but soon his head would be shaved as part of the ceremony. He cried out loudly, exuberantly, and when I turned to look at Nadira, she looked like she might faint.

Lisha grabbed Nadira's arm. "You will have to tell him how good-looking he was when you see him tonight at Fatima's." She was a classmate of ours whose dad was from America and owned a small safari lodge a few miles away, where white people from England or America or Holland stayed. Fatima was sometimes allowed to have friends over to the lodge, which had a small pool in the back.

Nadira shot me a look so quickly that no one else would have noticed.

"Everyone is going to Fatima's?" I asked the question even as I realized I shouldn't, even as I knew the answer and what it meant: I hadn't been included.

I wished I were used to this feeling of not fitting in. But it was like the itch of a mosquito bite, always there. So when the girls all eyed each other, I wanted to take my question back and let them off the hook. It was too late, though—I caught the nervous pity in their eyes. I turned and left before they could offer any weak excuses or, worse, invite me out of shame.

My mood plummeted faster than a white-headed vulture diving on a carcass. The dancing, the celebrations, the jubilation happening around me made me feel worse all of a sudden. I wandered around for a bit to see if I could shake it—it was supposed to be a happy day, after all—but after a while I decided to give up and head home early. I just hoped Momma was having a good time. She worked so hard, all day long. She deserved to have some fun.

I took the long way home, following the path that ran behind the school and edged up against the patch of forest. Even as I got farther away from the festivities, I still heard the distant laughter, taunting me.

EIGHT

The moon was out now, a golden glow against the violet sky, and the light danced against the glossy leaves of the trees. I was focused on watching the beautiful shadows when I was startled by voices. Or rather, one voice, loud and angry. I followed it and peered through a fence that surrounded a single house made of proper bricks like our school building. It was where the new game ranger lived. I followed the shouting to the backyard, instinctively crouching down to spy on what was happening.

A woman in a beautiful silk headscarf was screaming, "Please, Solo, please stop!"

I recognized her as Leku's mother. I'd seen her at the market a few times over the last few weeks—she was quiet and shy, smiling kindly at everyone, but that's about it. It was only a matter of time before Momma befriended her, because Momma befriended everyone.

Two little girls, Leku's younger sisters, were clutching her legs, their faces buried in either side of her skirt.

Meanwhile Solo's voice was thundering above everyone and everything. "How dare you disrespect me!" There was something in his eyes, a dark pleasure at making everyone, especially his son, cower.

Leku was on his knees, staring up at his father, defiant, but I could see the tremor in his hands, his fists shaking ever so slightly.

Solo Mungu had a thick stick in his hand. When he raised it into the air, I ran away as fast as I could. I couldn't bear to actually witness this punishment, even as I could all too clearly imagine the stick whipping through the air and striking Leku.

This cruel treatment of Leku by his father made me think of Baba. He would never lay his hands on me, and the sight of Momma crying would break his heart. What could Leku have done to deserve this treatment?

I tried to imagine what I could ever do to earn such rage from Baba or Momma and came up blank.

The rest of the way home, I wondered how Enkai up in the sky worked. He took away my baba, who was such a good man, but left babas such as Solo Mungu in the world, babas who did things that made their wives and daughters cry.

I took off my beautiful shuka and folded the fabric carefully, wondering when I would ever have a chance to wear it again. I lay on my mat staring at the ceiling waiting for the escape of sleep. My eyes were closed when Momma got home sometime later. I knew she had enjoyed herself because she hummed "Malaika" cheerily again as she prepared for bed. She could tell from my breathing that I was still awake, so she whispered, "Jama, did you enjoy yourself today?"

I thought about Nadira laughing and having fun without me, about the awful look on Leku's father's face, about how much I missed Baba. The thoughts piled up on me like so much dirt, like I could be buried under it all forever. I pretended to be asleep.

NINE

By Monday, I still hadn't shaken my dark cloud. I knew what I needed: to get to my special place, my secret place, the watering hole deep in the bush, where I was happiest.

But first I had to get through the school day. I spent the hours alternating between glancing at the clock and looking out the window, daydreaming.

Somehow I was still able to answer any question that Miss Mutua asked me. I am lucky that school comes easy for me, but that could be because I enjoy it so much. At least normally I did, but that day I was restless and antsy. As soon as Miss Mutua concluded our last lesson, I raced out of the building.

Most days the students gathered in front of the school to talk and play games before going home, and sometimes I joined Nadira and the girls who braided one another's hair and watched the boys play soccer. But I wasn't in the mood, and I definitely didn't want to hear all about the fun I missed at Fatima's.

Besides, it had been too long since I'd seen them, the elephants. *My* elephants. At least that's how I thought of them.

Before anyone noticed, I slipped down the path behind the school and practically broke into a jog. Behind the building was a big, open space of scattered red earth and then, past the clearing, a forest.

A path slipped between tree trunks. It wound its way down a small slope to the river, a long snake of water that stretched in either direction as far as the eye could see. This was where most of the town got water for food and washing.

The river was as far as I was technically allowed to go, but my destination was much deeper into the bush. It was twenty minutes on foot, over a large rocky hill and beyond. There wasn't a path, but I had carved out a way to walk between the shrubs.

I discovered this place back when Baba fell sick. He accidentally slashed through the palm of his hand with a sharp knife when he was cutting up pieces of cowhide to make me a new sleeping mat. It took eight days for the infection to take hold. The gash festered and pussed despite the poultices Momma painstakingly made and applied.

Momma couldn't—wouldn't—leave his side, so I was put in charge of her morning task, taking our big orange jerrican to fill with water. At eight years old, I could barely manage the empty can, let alone when it was filled with gallons of water. Carrying it made my small muscles shake and ache, but when you were determined, you did what you had to do. I would not let Momma down.

One day, though, before I retrieved water, I started wandering around, following an adorable little elephant shrew as he hopped around poking his hornlike snout into the dirt digging for beetles.

Before I realized it, I'd gone very far, too far. I was all alone, well beyond the boundaries of where Momma had said it was safe to venture. And I couldn't tell you how many times Momma drummed into my head the words *Jama, be safe.*

I should have been scared, but I was too distracted by what happened next. A herd of more than ten elephants emerged from over a ridge walking in a long, majestic line. I had seen elephants before, of course, but not so many together and not this close up.

They were the most beautiful animals, their soulful eyes taking in everything around them, their massive ears waving like flags in a soft wind. They lumbered slowly down to the shallow watering hole, like they had all the time in the world.

From behind a tree, I spied on them, mesmerized. I loved most how they communicated with one another. Sometimes out loud, sometimes silently, but it was clear that a connection was passing between them.

I watched them for as long as I could before racing back to the river and getting home.

TEN

For a time after Baba died, I didn't go back to the watering hole—I was too sad to do anything. But one day, I returned.

I knew Momma would kill me if she found out, but I also knew that she was so distracted by her crying and missing Baba that she might not notice.

It was a place where I could escape and no one looked at me like I was breaking. I could cry as much as I wanted, and I could talk to Baba out loud without anyone thinking I was strange. I would sit at the water's edge or pace around the shore and sob and yell as loud as I wanted. There was no need to feel embarrassed since there were only the trees to hear me. I started going as often as I could.

And that's how I got to be friends with the elephants. Sometimes they would be at the watering hole every day for weeks, and then sometimes they would be gone, off to roam other parts of the park. Over time, they got used to me being there with them, coming closer and closer until I could sit near enough to touch them, though I still hadn't dared. They weren't afraid of me at all. They understood I wasn't one of the men with the big guns come to kill them and take their tusks.

It was crazy, but I started to feel like I was one of them. Like if I got lost and couldn't go home, I could stay with them and I would be safe. It made me laugh to think of it—Jama Anyango, elephant girl.

Of course, I had to give all my friends names. The leader of the group I called Shaba. She was like Momma, strong and serious, but friendly. And there was Lulu and Tabia and Bawa, too. Most people might think all elephants look alike, but I could tell them apart easily: the extra-deep wrinkles on Modoc's knee. The deep scar that went along Bawa's backside, probably from fighting with another giant bull elephant. The way Loasa's tail was shorter than everyone else's.

Sometimes I would watch the elephants spraying themselves with water to cool off or wandering from bush to bush to munch on leaves, which is what took up most of their time, considering they ate between two hundred and four hundred pounds of food every day.

I always felt better on the occasions I talked to them. I could say things that I couldn't even say to Nadira, my voice becoming background noise among the bird cries and the soft splashes of water. Which is why I hoped, more than anything, the elephants with their calm reassurance would be there today.

ELEVEN

Even at my fast pace, it still took about fifteen minutes to make it to the watering hole. I slowed down as I got near because if the herd was already there, I didn't want to spook them. Other than the crunch of my footsteps, it was so quiet.

My stomach fell when I didn't see the elephants at the water, but I settled in to wait at my usual spot with my back up against a large acacia tree, its branches giving me much-needed shade from the sweltering sun. The amazing acacia tree can be massive, but its leaves are tiny, shaped like a slightly bigger and flatter grain of rice, except green, of course.

As I watched the leaves dance and a long train of blood-colored ants march up the bark, I already felt happier, like the bad feelings had left my body and been carried away with the barely there breeze. I told myself it would be okay if the elephants didn't come today, even though I longed for my friends.

Just then a familiar loud rustling broke through the silence. It sounded like, well, a herd of elephants. They materialized from the trees as if they had been there all along and only then decided to be seen.

Lulu, Bawa, Modoc! I was so happy to see them.

I got up and approached slowly, stepping onto a flat stone that was partially submerged so I could be close to the elephants as they trudged down to the water line.

Lulu greeted me with a loud trumpet, and then Bawa offered a snorting welcome. Bawa only visited the herd to mate or to check in on his babies, so he was extra excited to see me. His trunk swayed side to side like a greeting. Usually it was Shaba leading the herd, but she stayed behind with another female elephant.

I stood on tiptoes to get a better look at Shaba and see if she would come forward, and that's when I saw it! There, nestled under her legs, was the baby elephant I'd seen being born a few weeks ago. She looked like a mini Shaba.

I clapped my hands with delight, startling Lulu. I guessed the baby was a girl because her back was curvy, and Kokoo Naserian once told me that female elephants tend to have curvier spines. Since I'd seen her on her very first day of life, the little one had grown to about three feet tall. She wasn't fully steady on her feet and looked like her wrinkly skin, her feet, and her ears were still too big for her yet.

In the years I'd known this herd, there'd never been an infant, but given that it takes two years for a mother to carry one, that made sense.

Shaba gently nudged the baby toward the water, her trunk resting on its back.

I tentatively stepped across a few more stones in the watering hole so that I could get a better look. The elephants were, as usual, not alarmed. Quite the opposite—they seemed happy to see me, looking over at me and "speaking elephant," soft squeaks and rumbles. I did my best to mimic it and say some version of *congratulations* in their language.

Then we were all quiet for a bit, enjoying the moment. The adults snacked on leaves and drank water, but the baby watched me the whole time. Suddenly, she took a few steps toward me and a few steps more. Shaba watched her closely but didn't try to stop her. I realized the closer and closer the baby came, the tighter I was holding my breath, until she was so close I could actually touch her. My heart raced...with excitement, not fear.

Slowly, she extended her small trunk toward me as if asking me to touch it. I didn't want to do the wrong thing, so I copied her motion by extending my arm. At this, she moved her trunk to meet me. It was almost as if we were shaking hands. When she let out a small, pleasant squeak, I knew I had done the right thing, and I giggled along with her.

Her ears, too big for her baby head, flapped excitedly. I patted the tufts of black hair that extended from her head down along her back, and she let out a soft rumble, almost like a purr. The sparkle in her eyes and the pink tongue hanging goofily from her open mouth let me know she was enjoying this as much as I was.

I was in the middle of one of the most incredible and exciting experiences of my life. I only wished that I could freeze time.

All of a sudden, the baby lunged toward me clumsily. I put my arms out to steady her with a tight embrace. Though she was small, she was unimaginably strong. The problem was she didn't know it yet.

I held her tight and brought her down to the ground with me, making sure that we were eye to eye and her enthusiasm wouldn't lead to her accidentally trampling me. Without giving a second thought to my school uniform, I collapsed into the thick mud, and she draped her trunk over my legs. She looked so adorable and ridiculous that I laughed out loud.

Shaba sauntered closer and extended her long trunk to nudge her baby off me. She wrapped her long trunk around her baby's belly to lift her off me. She then offered her sturdy trunk, and I used it to lift myself up.

I felt so happy, I had chills up my arms. I still couldn't believe what had just happened. It was one of those moments where you look around and wonder if you're in a dream.

The baby looked so small next to her towering, mighty relatives, like a little brown bean or a seed. I knew exactly what I would call her.

"Until we meet again, Mbegu," I said quietly, giving her a name I thought fit her well. Mbegu, Swahili for *seed*, because just like one, she would grow, bloom, and flourish.

As the elephants retreated, I realized I could no

longer see their shadows on the ground, nor my own. I had lost myself and all track of time in this magical moment. Since forever, Momma had insisted that wherever I was, I had to have my shadow with me when I got back home.

No shadow meant the sun had set, and I was late and in big trouble.

TWELVE

I raced home even faster than I got to the watering hole, running so quickly that I stumbled and fell more than once. When I finally got to our manyatta, I had to take a moment outside our hut to catch my breath.

From inside, I heard a woman's voice. When I recognized it as belonging to Momma's friend Busara Kandenge, I felt relieved. While she was visiting, Momma was unlikely to tell me off about coming home without my shadow.

Busara Kandenge was the third and youngest wife of the man who owned the most cattle in our village.

While most of us were the color of the sky at night, her skin was light brown. Her voice was low and smooth like peanut butter. Everything about her was smooth. She didn't walk through the world so much as glide, tall and straight as if she had unlimited time.

When I heard her mention my name, I leaned in to listen.

"A man will help you raise Jama. She's a beautiful, intelligent child, but *eeish*, she's too much like a boy. A man will help you tame her."

I could hear the exasperation in Momma's voice when she spoke. "When my husband died, everyone said I needed a man to look after me and help me run the business. It's been four years. The business has even expanded. We're selling more sandals today than we were then. So what looking after do I need? I'm not convinced a man will change Jama's character. Besides, I like my Jama just the way she is."

Well done, Momma! I thought, my ear pressed against the rough mud wall to help my eavesdropping.

Yet Busara Kandenge was not finished. "But didn't you just say you were worried because she is detaching herself more and more from her friends?" she asked. "Didn't you just acknowledge that she's different?"

"Naturally, as a mother, I would prefer that she felt close to her people and fit in more. But I know she's a strong girl and she's very mature for her age," Momma said.

"Mature?" Busara Kandenge said. "Aluna, she's still climbing trees. In my day at her age, we were getting ready for marriage."

"Busara, she's not even turned thirteen. Girls mature at different times in different ways. My only worry is that if something ever happened to me, she would have no one."

"All the reason to allow the elders to find you a responsible husband. You are still young enough to bear more children, and then you won't have to worry about Jama being alone if something happened to you."

Momma laughed. "Oh, Busara, I thought you had stopped this marriage talk. Hamadi was my husband, and no one else will do. As for more children, that is even more—"

Then Busara Kandenge cut Momma short and said something in a low voice. I tried to step even closer to the hut so that I could hear, but my foot knocked the metal bucket I used for milking our old goat into the wall.

"Jama?"

I jumped away from the wall and dashed around to the entrance.

"Yes, Momma," I said, entering the room. I knew if Momma discovered that I was eavesdropping on her conversation she would be very angry.

"Hello, Auntie Busara, how are you?" I asked brightly, hoping to convince them that I had just arrived.

The two women looked at me wide-eyed. "What happened?" Their voices were a chorus.

Busara Kandenge turned to Momma and gave her a look that said, *You see what I mean?*

It was only then I remembered that I was covered in mud, courtesy of Mbegu.

"Where have you been? How did you get so dirty?" Momma asked, clearly displeased.

Think fast, Jama. "I tripped and fell on the path on the way home from school."

I knew better than to tell her that rather than staying late at school for extra work, I had been deep in the bush, sitting in a mud bath with a baby elephant. As if she would have believed that anyway. Remembering the weight of Mbegu's warm trunk on my lap made the stab of guilt I felt worth it.

THIRTEEN

I hated lying to Momma, but if she knew I was going so far to the watering hole most days after school, she would be very angry, so the lies continued.

Some days I told her I was staying after school to work on an extra project, and some days I said I was spending time with Nadira, helping in her mom's fruit stall at the market. At least twice a week, I did go right home after school to help Momma with making sandals or to cook dinner.

Those days I was preoccupied, missing Mbegu and wondering what she was up to. She was growing so fast, already a few inches taller in just a few weeks, so that she now couldn't fit under Shaba any longer. She was also much bolder and more curious, venturing farther away from her mother's cautious eye to explore the world around her.

Each day that I stayed home and didn't see the herd was a day I worried that they would be gone when I got back. Today was one of those days. I had come right home after school to help Momma make sandals, but I was distracted thinking about what Mbegu was doing that very moment. Her favorite new trick was to roll in the thick sludge at the watering hole's edge so that the mud sprayed into the air and rained down on her—and me if I wasn't careful.

The ache of missing someone I loved was a familiar feeling. At least I would be able to see Mbegu again.

"You're antsy today. Is everything okay?" Momma asked as she sewed colorful beads onto the leather that would become sandals. It was hard and painstaking work, using a large needle to pierce through the thick hide and add small stone after stone, but the results were beautiful. The man in Nairobi who sold the sandals for Momma said they were one of his most popular items, especially with tourists. I liked to imagine all our handmade shoes walking all over the world...England, Brazil, China, all the places I learned about in my schoolbooks and might like to go one day.

"I'm fine." I answered Momma's question with a shrug. I jabbed the needle into the leather far less gracefully than she did.

"You don't sound convincing," said Momma. "You've been awfully quiet, distracted, the last few weeks. You don't have your usual stories and complaints from school. I haven't heard a peep from you about how Miss Mutua's math lessons are boring or about Lisha trying to look over at your paper during tests, about the new boy who is always fighting...." Momma pretended to run out of breath.

I found myself smiling. "So you don't enjoy my stories?" I asked.

"Oh, I do! Just as much as you enjoy telling them. Which is why I miss them."

I wanted to tell Momma all about Mbegu then, of course—my very best story—but I couldn't because I knew she would forbid me from going to visit her.

"What about your friends?" Momma asked.

"What about them?"

"How are they doing? How's Nadira? I haven't seen her mother since the Eunoto, come to think of it."

"Nadira is fine. The girls are fine."

"But...?" Momma prodded.

"But nothing." I shrugged again. The sting of being left out was another thing I didn't want to tell Momma. The secrets I was keeping from her were piling up, which made me feel like there was something heavy in my stomach because Momma was the person I was closest to in the whole world.

"Are you and Nadira okay?"

"We're fine."

"Do you feel a little bit like you're growing apart sometimes?" Momma looked at me as she continued to stitch perfectly without a glance at her sewing.

"How did you know?" I wasn't actually surprised, though; Momma always could read my mind.

FOURTEEN

L et me guess," Momma said. "These days Nadira
likes to talk about boys and neck beads, but you
find that conversation boring."

"Is it wrong to prefer nature and animals over
boys?"

"It isn't wrong. The age you're at, some of your
friends are going to start thinking about boys before
you do. It will make you feel like you have less in common with them; it's natural. If I'm honest, I've seen a
change in Nadira that I haven't seen in you yet."

I wondered what Momma meant by a change, but I
felt too shy to ask.

She went on. "Don't worry too much about it. People develop at different ages. The distance you feel between you and Nadira will close up soon when you are more mature. It will happen in time," Momma said, reaching across and patting my hand reassuringly.

I was silent for a moment, trying to work out how to speak my heart. When I finally spoke, it was in a quiet voice. "But...but what if I grow up and still don't want to just cook and sew for my husband? What if I want something else, Momma?"

She put down her sewing when she looked at me. "Oh, Binti, trust me, you will feel different when you are older and you meet someone special. When that day comes, all the negative thoughts you have about marriage will vanish in a flash and it won't seem like such a bad idea."

I crinkled my nose at the thought, and Momma burst out laughing. "Jama, that face! Marriage can be a good thing. Look at me and your baba."

"That's different."

"How? If I thought like you do, I would not have married him."

I thought about that for a minute. Maybe if I could meet someone like Baba...but not one of the boys I knew was as kind, as smart, as funny. They didn't listen to me the way Baba listened to Momma—like he really wanted to hear what she was saying. Besides, I still wanted to do more than get married. I wanted to travel and to learn, too, but I didn't know anyone, especially any women, who had done that.

"I just don't want to be stuck, Momma. I want to have a big life." I didn't know what exactly that meant, but I knew the words were true.

Momma reached out and grabbed my hand, which was dotted with tiny pinpricks of blood from the sharp sewing needle. "I want you to be happy, Jama. I know it's important to be true to yourself and not to follow what others say. But at the same time the reality is that no one can survive alone. We need family and our community to survive. We need to connect to our roots and culture because it makes us who we are. I just ask that you remember that, okay?"

I nodded to make her happy, but the truth was I was okay being alone, as long as I had Mbegu…and Momma.

Momma squeezed my hand. "I don't want you to become isolated and lonely, Binti. Your baba has been gone for four years, and when it's my time to go, I don't want you to be left without any family."

"Momma!" I put my hands over my ears. "How can you even say something like that?"

"*Binti.*" She took my hands away from my ears. "Everyone has their time. I don't want to alarm you, but it's my job to prepare you for things that can happen in life. Life is such that loved ones part; they separate—no one is together forever. If something happens to me, I want you to have the support of friends and community. Otherwise you'll be alone."

"Oh, Momma, please don't...don't say things like that."

Now it was my eyes that were glassy.

FIFTEEN

She was just as excited to see me as I her. I swear Mbegu almost tripped, she darted over so fast when I got to the watering hole today. Like she was a puppy and not a baby elephant.

The rest of the herd was standing in the brown water, which was very smart since it was a hot day, like a fire was at your back. Sweat leaked down the sides of my face. I wanted to sink into the cool water myself, but of course I knew better. So I settled for sitting on the fallen tree and watching Mbegu take giant sips. As she did, I chatted about my day as usual.

"Do you think I will get an A, Mbegu?" I asked

after I told her about my surprise math test that afternoon. I knew the answer was probably yes; I could envision the perfect marks when Miss Mutua returned our graded papers tomorrow. Mbegu's answer was to spray me with her trunk.

I laughed in surprise and took it to mean she agreed. I hoped my uniform would have time to fully dry before I got home. I thought about taking my shirt off and hanging it on a tree, but even all alone, I was too modest to do so. I settled for fanning it, so I didn't notice right away that the elephants had become agitated.

Shaba let out a trumpet, and Mbegu knew just what her mother meant: *Come here.* They moved closer together, and then became very still all of a sudden, on high alert. I felt their fear; it was contagious.

I ducked behind the tree I'd been sitting on, looking around for danger. Maybe a lion? It was very quiet, not even a breeze to shake the leaves. All I could hear was my heartbeat like thunder in my ear.

And then I saw him. A man I had never seen. Across the watering hole, standing behind some bushes. He was watching the herd from a couple of yards away. I crouched even lower. If I moved, he would notice me.

The sweat on my skin had turned cold. I was more

afraid of a strange man than I would be of a lion. *Who is this person?*

I noticed then the gun slung over his shoulder. The KWS carried guns, but he wasn't wearing a uniform. He was wearing a black shirt and pants. When he turned his left cheek toward me, I could see a long, raised scar like a thick white rope cutting through his dark skin. It ran all the way from his forehead to his chin.

A sense of dread creeped up my spine. There were no good reasons for him to be in the forest with a gun watching the elephants, only bad ones.

As if hearing a silent cue, the elephants turned as one and quickly moved away from the watering hole, away from the man. Just as quickly, the man disappeared deeper into the bush, away from the village, thank Enkai.

I took a deep breath to calm my nerves and got up to head in the opposite direction, toward home, but my body still felt shaky. The heat felt like it was trapping me, and the quiet I usually found so peaceful felt sinister. The trees towering over me were threatening.

My eyes darted around, and every once in a while I glanced back over my shoulder, Momma's voice in my ear: *Be safe, Jama.*

When I heard a rustling in the bushes, I convinced myself it was my imagination, my fear talking. I stopped to listen but heard nothing and started to walk again. That's when he jumped out from behind a tree in front of me.

"Mmmaaaaaaaa!" A loud scream erupted from my mouth and echoed all around the trees.

"Jama, Jama. It's only me."

SIXTEEN

Leku stood before me with a big smile on his face. I had never seen him with anything but a scowl, so he looked pretty odd.

He was obviously pleased with himself for having frightened me. He was still in his school uniform, the gray-and-pink-checked shirt soiled, the breast pocket hanging loosely. It must have ripped during yet another fight at school.

"You short little fool! Why did you scare me?" I glared at him. I knew calling him short was as good as punching him in the face, which I felt like doing. Being teased about his height made him angry and was one of the reasons he was always fighting in school.

"I'm not a fool and I'm not short," he said, the smile vanishing from his face and his eyes narrowing, as if he hadn't expected me to talk back to him.

"You are both. Only fools go around scaring people and fighting everyone for no reason," I said, my heart still pounding from the scare he had given me.

"And you are crazy," he snarled. "You talk to elephants."

I was angry to discover he had been following me, that he had been spying on me at the watering hole. My cheeks warmed with embarrassment. *How long has he been watching me?* I started to walk past him, but he blocked my path.

I bunched my fists and held them up like I had seen him do at school. "Get out of my way," I said, in what I believed was a threatening tone. "I'm not one of those weak boys you fight at school. I'm not scared of you." I looked him straight in the face and hoped I sounded convincing.

"Okay, elephant girl."

"And don't call me that." I started to walk, and he fell in step beside me.

"Why not? You seem to love the elephants."

I stopped walking and turned to stare at him. "How long have you been following me? Watching me?"

"Long enough." His voice was softer now, and his smile returned so that I noticed for the first time the slight gap between his two front teeth.

"Well, I like elephants, and you're not going to make me feel bad about it," I said.

"I like them, too. They're kind and they don't eat other animals."

This caught me off guard. I almost stopped in my tracks again. Leku was being nice and was capable of liking something, and he actually knew about elephants.

"Did you know an elephant drinks fifty gallons of water a day?" he asked, clearly proud of this knowledge.

I did know, but was surprised he did.

"Yes, I know that." I was still trying to make sense of this confusing boy when we got to the entrance gate of the reserve. We spotted a dirty Land Rover parked in a small clearing between trees. It had the emblem of the Kenya Wildlife Service on the side, and Leku's dad was in the driver's seat. It was impossible to tell if he saw us given his dark glasses, but Leku's smile disappeared and he looked very serious again.

"That's my father," he said.

"I know." I thought about Leku on the ground under his towering dad, shaking.

"He is here to catch the poachers. In Namibia he caught three men...."

As he went on, I thought about interrupting to tell him about the man in the woods. Maybe he could report it to his dad. The idea of telling Solo Mungu myself made my knees shake.

"Everyone is scared of him," Leku was saying now, echoing my silent thoughts.

"Are *you* scared of him?"

He looked sideways at me. "What do you mean?"

"Well, you said *everyone* is scared of him."

"I meant the poachers, the bad guys. They are scared because he catches them, because he is brave and fearless. My baba is the best."

"He may be fearless. But is he a good baba?"

A cloud passed over his face. "He *is* a good baba."

"I saw him yelling at you...the night of the Eunoto," I blurted out. "A good baba does not frighten his son and make his wife cry."

As soon as the words escaped my mouth, his eyes popped open and he lunged at me. I squealed and he stopped himself, frozen in place with balled fists. He wagged his forefinger close to my face. "Iwee, don't ever talk about my baba like that! You crazy elephant girl," he snarled. "Baba is a good man."

With that, he stomped off.

SEVENTEEN

Where have you been going after school?" Kokoo Naserian glared at me as I milked our old goat.

I shouldn't have been surprised that she knew I had been lying. Momma might have been distracted by her work, but Kokoo Naserian knew everything that happened in our village. Even with her bad vision, nothing got past her eagle eye, so I didn't even bother to protest. Besides, I longed to tell someone about seeing Mbegu yesterday.

"I've been going to a watering hole deep in the reserve. It's the most beautiful place. And there's an elephant herd there—with a baby."

Just thinking about Mbegu made me smile. I waited for Kokoo Naserian to chastise me. Instead, always full of surprises, she smiled. "How many are in the herd?" she asked.

I should have known that Kokoo Naserian would understand. She loved animals as much as I did. She was known to hold her chickens in her lap and lovingly pet them.

"About twelve or so," I told her.

She nodded approvingly. "That is a lot. For these times. When I was your age, the herds were hundreds strong. We sometimes would have to wait hours for them to pass. You could feel the rumble of the earth when they were a great distance away, that's how many there were." Kokoo Naserian looked off into the distance as if she could see the old days playing on a screen.

I was about to tell her the many stories I was bursting with about Mbegu when we heard the loud horn blowing from town. There were different horn sounds for different things. This one announced an urgent meeting.

"I wonder what's happened?" I said.

A neighbor woman carrying a large basket on her

head walked by our boma just then and called out. "Did you hear?"

"No, what happened?" I asked, my heart revving.

"They got an elephant—the poachers killed one in the middle of the night."

My stomach dropped. I collapsed to the ground and accidentally kicked over the bucket of milk. The warm liquid spilled all over the red dirt, leaving a dark puddle. I didn't care about the wasted milk; all I could think of were my friends...Shaba, Lulu, Modoc...*Mbegu*.

What if one of them was dead? The ringing in my ears was so loud, I almost didn't hear Kokoo Naserian, who stood over me now.

"Are you okay? Come, come, let's get you inside."

"No," I said to her, gathering my wits about me. "We have to get to town. I need to know what happened."

Momma was already in the village, having left at the crack of dawn to get to the markets early when there were the freshest fruits, so we would meet her there.

I could tell that Kokoo Naserian felt my impatience and was walking as fast as she could, her walking stick tapping the ground like a scorpion scurrying, but it still wasn't very fast. By the time we got to the schoolyard, Laibon Umoja was standing by the school bell on a small wooden platform made of stacked packing crates, addressing the crowd.

"It is with a heavy heart that I report the unfortunate events of last night," he said. "A gang of poachers approached an elephant herd a few miles away. One animal was shot and killed."

I thought of the man I'd seen a few weeks back, dressed in black, with a gun, watching the elephants. Surely it was not a coincidence. *Why did I not say anything? I know why. I was afraid of getting in trouble. And that fear may have cost the life of one of the elephants.* I let out a distraught cry, and Kokoo Naserian squeezed my hand.

There were a few metal folding chairs near the market stalls, and I ran over to grab one for Kokoo since she wasn't able to stand for long. She shooed it away at first because she did not like anyone to call attention to her limitations, but after one hundred years on this earth, surely it was not a shame to have a seat.

"These men are ruthless killers," the laibon went on, "and so the concern that they may still be nearby is understandable. It is important for us now to take cautionary measures. As you know, it is not uncommon for elephants to become wild and frantic when startled by poachers. They are known to stampede recklessly, which in a few instances has tragically led to human death. I ask that you be extra cautious and keep a vigilant eye out when it comes to the elephants and the poachers, who may still be in the area."

I knew the laibon meant well, but I resented the implication that it was the elephants we must be wary of, that it was the elephants that may hurt us, when they were nothing but the victims in the situation.

The laibon then called upon Solo Mungu to address the crowd. He was standing just to the right of the laibon with two men on his team, who were wearing brown KWS polo shirts and khaki pants. They looked like a mix between stern soldiers and zookeepers, which I suppose they sort of were in a way.

But where was Solo Mungu when the poachers were terrorizing the elephants, and why didn't he stop them? Leku's words rang in my ear. *Baba is a good man. Everyone is scared of him.*

Even his own son, I thought, remembering Solo Mungu lording over Leku with that glint of satisfaction in his eyes.

EIGHTEEN

Solo Mungu stepped onto the wooden platform and pulled up the thick belt that cut deeply into the middle of his body, giving him the shape of the number eight. I couldn't shake the feeling that he was hiding behind his usual dark sunglasses.

"Poachers are very crafty and tenacious people. It takes experience and intelligence to catch them. But we are succeeding at arresting them. Make no mistake, I will find whoever did this," he said, his voice booming with authority.

When he finished speaking, there was applause.

The laibon opened the floor for questions, and Kokoo Naserian held up her walking stick. When Laibon Umoja nodded his head at her, a few disgruntled murmurs rippled through the crowd; he hushed them by raising his long arms.

Kokoo Naserian struggled to stand up and shuffle a few steps to the front of the crowd. She gritted her teeth in determination and then faced the crowd. "We have a saying: There is no gecko that does not claim to have the longest tail. So someone claiming to be the best of all rangers is of no merit or value to us." A few giggles and another wave of disgruntled murmurs spread through the crowd. "Of late I have seen strange cars driving around the reserve. Who are these people? How can you say you are protecting the elephants when you do not patrol?" Kokoo Naserian asked, to applause as well as jeers.

"Kokoo, we know your eyesight is not the best these days, but I will tell you that there are more patrols now than ever before!" Solo Mungu shouted from where he had perched his gigantic body on a small wooden stool.

"You can laugh at my being old. But I see what I see. And I know what I know. Just remember, coal laughs at ashes not knowing the same fate will befall it," she hit back with another proverb.

Solo Mungu stood up and yanked off his sunglasses. "Perhaps our grandmother here does not understand that poachers were here last night shooting with big guns. We risked our lives to chase them away. This is war, and our grandma is accusing us of not doing our work?" he asked, beady eyes blazing.

"What I am saying is that if it's a war against poachers, you are losing because elephants are still getting killed," said Kokoo Naserian, who was drowned out by increasing jeers from the crowd.

When Laibon Umoja hushed the crowd, she spoke again. "Let me also say that the elephants realized they are being hunted during the day so they started moving at night to protect themselves. The poachers therefore have to poach at night to find the elephants," she said, stabbing the ground with her walking stick to emphasize her point. "The elephants are learning to protect themselves, but it is up to us to help them. It's the right thing to do and good for everyone."

Kokoo Naserian has always stressed how important it is for us to live in harmony with the animals around us. We are no better or worse than any wild creature, so we have to share our resources and lands with them.

Solo Mungu shook his head at her words. "What are you saying, Kokoo? That elephants have intelligence?"

"Yes! That is exactly what I'm saying. They are more intelligent than you!" Kokoo Naserian pointed her walking stick at the man.

Laughter erupted from the crowd, which only made Solo angrier. He took a deep breath as if trying to calm down, but the sharp edge was still in his voice when he spoke.

"Laibon, with all due respect, we are here to discuss serious matters. Not the intelligence of elephants. And let us remember that elephants have been known to attack people, too. This is why our job is so dangerous—threats all around. My men and I deserve proper respect."

The crowd started talking among themselves, nodding and shaking their heads at what was being said.

"These animals deserve respect, too. They only attack when they feel threatened," said Kokoo. "In the past it was very rare to hear of an elephant attacking humans because we stayed out of each other's way. We did not kill them in large numbers to satisfy our greed. In the past—"

The crowd did not let Kokoo Naserian finish her sentence. Many booed and waved at her to sit down. The old woman was shaky and spent by this point, so I grabbed her arm to steady her and help her back down in the chair. I was shocked by her passionate speech, and where she got the energy to deliver it, but that's just how much Kokoo Naserian loved the elephants.

Just then I heard Momma's voice, cutting through the mayhem. "People, people..." She clapped her hands sharply, twice. The crowd started to quiet down when they realized it was Momma asking for their attention.

"My people, we are here to discuss a problem that affects all of us. The contribution each and every one of us makes to the discussion is important. Kokoo Naserian has been here longer than any one of us. She has lived with the elephants for many years. Let us listen to what she has to say. Let us learn. And please, let us have respect for our Kokoo Naserian. She is brave enough to say what many of us think. Some of you may not agree or like what she says, but it is her opinion and she has the right to express it."

The crowd clapped and cheered in approval. It was amazing how Momma turned the tide in Kokoo Naserian's favor. But it wasn't Momma I was looking at, because Leku had caught my eye. He was standing next to her, staring right at me. The expression on his face was hard to read. When I looked back at his father's face, though, the expression was crystal clear: fury shone in his eyes.

NINETEEN

Those eyes were still haunting me later that night when I was tossing and turning, knowing sleep wouldn't come. I wouldn't be able to relax until I knew the elephants were okay, but I also knew I would never convince Momma to let me go into the bush after dark.

After I was sure Momma was deep in slumber, I quietly snuck out of the manyatta. I needed to walk off my restlessness under the moon and the stars and to pray to Enkai that Mbegu was okay. I wandered down the path toward school.

Suddenly, the sound of a car engine broke into the

quiet of the night, coming from someplace distant off the path, which was rare at this late hour. Then I heard the engine of another car.

Curious, I followed the sound deeper and deeper into the bush. I spotted two stopped vehicles facing each other among the trees set far back from the road. I recognized the Land Rover—it belonged to Solo Mungu. The other car was a black pickup truck.

I slowly and quietly walked closer and shimmied up the trunk of a nearby tree, camouflaging myself among the branches. In the cover of darkness, no one would see me.

From my perch, I watched Solo Mungu emerge from his vehicle. He walked over to the driver's-side window of the truck. I peered closely at the driver, illuminated by the Land Rover's headlights. The light caught his cheek and I gasped. There it was, the angry scar cutting through his face. There was no mistaking it. It was him! It was the man I saw in the woods.

I scooted out farther on a branch and leaned in to hear their conversation.

"Do you have it?" Solo Mungu barked into the truck's open window.

The man was silent; he just handed Solo something.

It was an envelope, which Solo opened. He pulled out a fan of money and counted.

"This is only half of what we agreed to," Solo Mungu barked.

"Yes, yes, you get the rest tomorrow. We need one more kill and then we will go."

One more kill.

My heart started racing as I put two and two together. It was as clear as the night sky: the poachers were paying Solo Mungu to look the other way! His one job was to protect the elephants. Instead…I couldn't even finish the thought, I was so upset.

The men shook hands and then laughed about something.

I couldn't take another second. I started backing down the tree trunk, but my foot caught on a branch, and I watched in horror as my sandal fell to the ground.

I froze in fear for a second as the men whipped their heads to look up at the same time.

"Who's there?" Solo Mungu's shout rang through the air.

TWENTY

I sprang into action, clambering down the tree trunk at top speed and jumping to the ground as soon as I was close enough to get down without breaking a leg. Then I took off as fast as I could, slashing with my arms at the leaves and branches that blocked my way. I could hear the men shouting.

At some point I lost my other sandal. I knew I was creating a good distance between myself and the men because I couldn't hear them behind me anymore. Then it dawned on me that once I got back to the path, the open space would give me away. The men would see me no matter how far behind they were.

The thought almost stopped me in my tracks, but I carried on running. I would think of something when I got nearer to the bottom of the hill. Perhaps I could hide until sunrise.

Then, just when I thought my heart couldn't pound any harder, I heard footsteps. Someone was catching up with me. A wave of fear rose in my throat. I thought I was going to throw up. I was running my fastest, but the pounding of feet behind me was getting closer— then I heard a voice.

"Don't scream. Don't scream."

Before I could place the voice, a body crashed into me, and we tumbled to the ground. In the split second before we rammed into the base of an enormous baobab tree, I realized who my accoster was.

TWENTY-ONE

S shhhhhh…" Leku held his index finger to his lips.

Not that I could say anything if I wanted to. I was breathless and my shoulder, which took the brunt of the impact, felt as if it were on fire.

Leku gestured for me to follow him into a dugout pit behind the tree. It was just big enough for both of us to fit facing each other with our knees touching and hunched up to our faces. The smell of fresh soil tickled my nostrils.

I could hear heavy crunching on dry leaves and undergrowth nearby even over the loud pounding in my ears. I stared wide-eyed at Leku, who raised his finger to his lips again.

"Who was it?" Solo Mungu asked.

"It's a girl's shoe," the poacher said.

"I bet it's that crazy girl who behaves like a boy," Solo Mungu muttered.

"I saw a girl in the bush before, down where I saw the herd."

So he did see me! A sprinkle of goose bumps popped up all over my arms. I had never sat so still in my life. The voices were so close that I feared the men would hear my heart beating.

"I don't like it," Solo Mungu said.

"She is just a young girl, and she knows better than to say anything."

"She'd better not, if she knows what's good for her." Solo Mungu's terrifying tone brought a fresh wave of goose bumps.

We sat and listened to the men walk away. Then we sat a bit longer until we heard the vehicles drive off.

Silently, Leku stood up, and I scrambled out of the hole after him. He walked up to a tree with a forked trunk, and from the hollow where it split, Leku hauled out a brown sack. Placing it at his feet, he untied the knot and pulled out a pair of blue plastic sandals, which he silently handed to me. I suspected that when Leku skipped school, he spent his time at the tree, his special place like I had mine. Hence the sack with his stuff hidden away here.

My feet were throbbing from running barefoot, and my breath was still coming in short sharp bursts, so I put the sandals on, no questions asked.

I wanted to explain what I had seen, to see if Leku still thought his baba was a good baba, knowing he was in cahoots with the evil poachers, but he probably wouldn't believe me. *Will anyone?*

I needed proof. I could tell Momma, but it would mean revealing that I'd lied to her over and over. *It will mean I can never go to the watering hole again. I might never see Mbegu again.*

"Are you okay?" Leku's concerned voice broke through my thoughts.

"Yes," I lied. I was far from okay.

"I will walk you home."

"You don't need to do that." But that was another lie; I was happy to have Leku's company.

"Why are you always following me?" I asked him.

"I'm not!" He sounded like I had just offered the greatest insult.

"But you were in the woods...and you were out tonight?"

"Don't flatter yourself, Jama. You're not the only one who likes to go on walks. Or who can't sleep at night. It was a coincidence."

But the way he said it...I wasn't so sure. Either way, the coincidences worked in my favor.

I was grateful he was there that night. I told him so when we got near my manyatta, and he stared at me like there was something more to say.

I met the silence with a wave goodbye and then snuck inside, where Momma, thank Enkai, remained fast asleep. I crawled into bed, resolving that I would have to tell her everything in the morning. Even if it meant confessing that I'd been lying, it was the only way to get justice and protect the elephants.

Despite the thick heat of the night, I shuddered thinking about that conversation, and even more when I remembered Solo Mungu's words: *If she knows what's good for her.*

TWENTY-TWO

lthough I woke up the next morning with my feet still throbbing from all the running, as soon as the sun came up, I offered to go with Momma to fetch water and do the washing.

Unlike milking the goat, which I didn't mind, I hated the weekly washing. We would carry heavy baskets of clothes down to the river to wash and then carry back the wet clothes—which were even heavier with the weight of water—and hang them to dry in the sun.

At Fatima's father's lodge they had a big machine where you put all the clothes in and added soap. It made a loud noise and shook all the clothes around inside, and then they came out clean. And then there was a machine that blew hot air on the clothes like wind in a box.

I dreamed that we could have a machine like that to make weekly washing easier, but whenever I asked Momma, she told me to stop my complaining and that we didn't need machines to do what our capable hands could do.

I vowed I would not complain that day. I would earn some goodwill for being a helpful, dutiful daughter, and then I would tell her what I needed to. If all went well, maybe she would even be understanding enough that she would let me go into the bush and check on the herd.

The weight of my worry for them was heavier than the basket of dirty clothes on my head as we walked to the river. The morning sun had fully emerged, and the sky was as blue as sapphire. A small flock of long-tailed fiscals flew overhead, prompting Momma to hum the melody of "My Little Bird," a song she sang to me when I was little. The song evoked memories as warm and sweet as honey.

As we walked, various neighbors greeted us along the crowded path to the river.

"Good morning, Aluna, how are you?"

"Look at that clever daughter of yours. So dutiful."

"It's a beautiful day, is it not?"

Momma responded with waves and warm smiles. "We are well, by Enkai's grace."

I wanted to wait until we were at the river and had a quiet moment to tell Momma everything, but my stomach twisted in the meantime.

In my mind I rehearsed over and over what I would say. I knew Momma—once she got over being angry that I had lied to her, she would help me come up with a plan to stop Solo Mungu's evil ways.

As we got closer to the water, we could hear people's animated chatter. Usually there was talking or laughing or singing at the river on Saturday morning as many people gathered for their weekly chores, but right now the collective voices sounded . . . nervous.

Momma and I picked up our steps, and as we got closer to the water, we could see what had everyone's attention. Three elephants stood about a hundred yards away along the riverbank—Lulu, Shaba, and little Mbegu. They were alive! I was so relieved, I could have cried.

"Are you okay, Jama?" Momma looked at me, confused.

"Yes, yes, I am fine." I beamed.

"It's strange for the elephants to be over here, this close. I can't remember the last time I saw one here."

I couldn't believe my good fortune.

TWENTY-THREE

The elephants are likely spooked from the shooting," Momma said. "The herd must have gotten separated in the panic."

I watched them closely and noticed their behavior was different today. Mbegu looked small and scared, staying so close to Shaba that she was touching her at all times. I led Momma past our neighbors and along the river to get as close to the elephants as possible.

"What are you doing, Jama? Not any closer." Of course, Momma didn't know about my relationship with the herd. I couldn't exactly run over and hug Mbegu until I explained everything, and now was my chance. Momma dropped the jerricans and her basket and started plucking out dirty clothes and dunking them in the river, all the while keeping a wary eye on the elephants.

"Momma, I have something to tell you. I know these elephants." I stopped short of saying they were my friends because it already sounded a little crazy.

"What are you talking about, Jama?" She looked really confused now.

"I've...I've been visiting them, after school, deep in the hills of the reserve, where they usually stay." My voice was quiet, sheepish, and there was no mistaking the shock and anger in Momma's eyes as she registered what I was saying. She dumped the wet clothes she was scrubbing into the water and grabbed me by the shoulders.

"You saw them *where*?" Momma bent close to me. Our noses were almost touching.

I looked down.

"Jama, you know that is way out of bounds! I'm disappointed in you, Binti. At your age you should know to stick to rules for your own safety. I can't believe you would lie to me like this."

The angry look on her face was replaced with hurt, and that was far worse.

"Momma, I'm sorry. I know I shouldn't go past the river, but I feel safe and at peace there...I have this place I go...and..." I tried to explain how I could talk to the elephants, how my special spot made me feel. But it all came out in a jumble and I started crying.

Momma's face softened. She sat on a jerrican and motioned for me to do the same, so we were facing each other. "Jama, I understand. And I am happy that you have a place that makes you feel good. But if I'm angry with you, it's because I'm scared, scared that you might get hurt. It's not only about the animals harming you— what if you fell somewhere? How would I find you if you're in a place you're not supposed to be?"

Her eyes jumped to look over my shoulder, and she stood up, taking a step past me in the direction of the elephants.

I was getting ready to tell her all about Solo Mungu, but I looked up to see what had distracted her. The elephants had wandered even closer, much to my delight. I knew better than to think they would be close enough to touch because too many people were there.

Besides, something was wrong. I could tell immediately. Shaba was tense, flapping her ears and stomping her feet. I think she spotted me then and started approaching, but she stopped short. I started to walk toward her, but Momma blocked me with her arm.

"Sshhhhhh...she's agitated," Momma said, her voice hushed.

It made sense that Shaba was still unsettled from what happened the other night. How could she not be after the poachers killed one of their herd in cold blood?

"Keep still." Momma's breathing changed. She was panting nervously.

Shaba moved from side to side, her eyes fixed on us.

"Here, let me—" Again, I tried to take a few steps.

"No!" Momma interrupted me in an angry whisper. "Don't go near her—she's warning us."

TWENTY-FOUR

The fear in Momma's voice and on her face made my belly churn. I tried to recall what I knew about how to calm an elephant, but my mind went completely blank.

At that moment Shaba let out a loud trumpet. Then she shook her head, and her big ears flapped with a mighty *WHOOOOSH*, spraying loose sand and water everywhere.

I held my breath. This was not the same elephant that had held out her trunk to me and let me play with her baby.

"What should we do?" I asked quietly.

"Better to stand still. If we run, she will charge," Momma whispered back.

But even though we stood still, the elephant began to trot toward us. Her pace quickened, and along with it, my heartbeat; it drummed in my ears. I noticed that her tail was standing straight and her big ears were splayed out. To my horror, she tucked her trunk under her chin and started charging.

Momma had told me not to move, but all the will in the world wouldn't have kept me still. I started to run. It all happened so fast. As soon as I turned away, I heard the elephant's feet pounding toward us, and within seconds her big shadow fell upon us. From around me, I heard screams. Momma's loudest of all.

"Jama, move!" She knocked me out of the way. But not before I saw the elephant raise her trunk high up above Momma's body and let out another deafening trumpet. I closed my eyes tight because I couldn't bear to look.

My legs tangled under me, and I tripped and slammed into the red earth with a thump, the wind knocked out of me. My eyes were closed, but I heard another scream. It was followed by one heavy thud and Momma's shriek. Just one sharp cry. That pair of sounds, the thud and

Momma's yell, I knew even then, would haunt me for the rest of my life.

The world around me began to move in slow motion. I pulled myself up off the ground and saw Momma lying facedown. My heart froze in my chest, all the sounds around me switched off. All the sounds except my screaming at the top of my lungs at the sight of Momma's collapsed body.

She looked as if she were sleeping peacefully, but I knew something was very wrong. I wanted to shake her awake, but I was scared to touch her.

Shaba retreated but continued to pace back and forth at a distance, Mbegu underfoot. But I barely registered them. All my senses vanished from my body.

"No! No! No!" I wailed over and over between violent sobs. My wailing seemed to reach me from afar, like it was echoing all around me. Then I realized that's because it wasn't only me wailing, it was other people, too, forming one loud, collective cry.

I looked up and saw women and men around me, faces twisted in grief. Their horror-stricken expressions made it all too real. They had seen what I had: Momma lying in the red soil, life trampled out of her.

Shaba, how could you? The thought was a whisper that bounced around my brain.

"Aluna! Enkai, why Aluna? Please, no! Please, no, don't let it be true!" more voices wailed.

More people came running. I couldn't hear them, though, through the blood rushing in my ears and the loud pounding of my heart, which filled my head like the deafening drums of war. But even if I couldn't hear, I could read the painful truth on their lips.

"Aluna ameaga! Aluna ameaga!"

The reality of their words hit home. Aluna is dead.

TWENTY-FIVE

verything whirled around me. The sky, the river, the people, the elephants, the blood—it was a blur of blue and black and brown and red. I squeezed my eyes closed, shutting out the scene. I couldn't bear to face what had happened.

I didn't even know how much time had passed when I felt a soft warm palm wipe the tears from my face. I opened my eyes and looked into the face of Busara Kandenge. She was sitting in a crumpled heap beside me, her knees sinking into the damp earth. She spoke but her words sounded like gibberish punctuated with the name Aluna.

I watched her rise to her knees, untie her shuka, shake it open, and lay it over Momma's body. Suddenly the crowd backed away, and I turned to see Shaba move slightly closer to us. She picked her head up high and threw it back down again dramatically.

Panic gripped Busara Kandenge as she scrambled to her feet, reaching out to grab my sleeve. "The elephant is coming. Get up, Jama, you'll get trampled!" she screamed.

I tried to get up, but my legs wobbled like jelly so Busara Kandenge offered me both her hands. As I struggled to my feet, the roar of a car engine came closer and closer. A Kenya Wildlife Service Land Rover rumbled toward us and screeched to a halt. Two men stood up through the open roof. I recognized them as the same two that were standing with Solo Mungu when he addressed the village yesterday.

"What's happening?" the driver asked. The second man was bald and wore a green bandana on his head. Over their brown shirts, both wore bright yellow vests the color of Kokoo Naserian's baby chicks.

Someone from the crowd shouted angrily, "Can't you see that elephant has killed one of us? Why don't you shoot it?"

"Aluna, my Aluna is dead!" Busara Kandenge

rushed up to the Land Rover. "An elephant...look... she's stampeding. I don't know why. I don't know what happened."

Busara Kandenge was patting her chest with the palm of her hand as she spoke, as if to soothe the pain inside.

"She's clearly out of control," said the man with the bandana, assessing Shaba. "We have to shoot her." He gripped his tranquilizer gun and brought it to the ready.

"Are you sure?" asked the driver. "Let's get everyone out of here and give her a chance to calm down."

"No, no, her posture is too aggressive. I'm calling it."

Before I understood what was happening, the man aimed the gun and fired. There was a loud *crack* and within seconds, Shaba crashed to the ground with an earthshaking thud. I winced, retreating into Busara's arms. I looked up to see that Lulu had run away, but Mbegu had stayed right by her mother's body, quaking in fear.

"It's tranquilized." The driver spoke into a walkie-talkie attached to his vest and jumped out of the car as a faraway voice crackled back. But that didn't sound like a tranquilizer dart. That sounded like a bullet.

For a moment, everything was quiet, everyone silenced by shock. Then murmurs began humming as both men jumped from the car and pulled out a stretcher. The murmurs grew louder as the men approached Momma's body.

"*No!*" I hollered, grabbing at the air, kicking and screaming against Busara's arms, which held me tight. "Momma! Momma! *No! No! No!*"

"Where are you taking her?!" somebody called out.

The men didn't respond. They just looked at me with pity as they gently lifted Momma and laid her on the stretcher. Again I squeezed my eyes shut because I couldn't bear to see Momma under the blue cloth being carried away from me.

I opened my eyes again after a moment. The men had placed the stretcher in the back of the Land Rover, and now the man with the bandana walked over to Shaba, who was lying as still as Momma had been. But she was only tranquilized; she'd get back up.

Unlike Momma.

TWENTY-SIX

The grief, the fear, and the shock were a confusing tumble inside me, but one thing was clear: I still wanted Shaba to be okay. This wasn't her fault.

The driver walked over to Shaba's hulking gray frame lying on the ground, her massive legs in a limp pile.

He knelt, a concerned look on his face. "She's bleeding…a lot."

I looked over to see the giant pool of blood forming around her enormous body, suddenly spilling and then gushing, creating a fast-flowing stream.

The driver stood.

"What kind of gun did you use?" he asked his partner with urgency. "Why didn't you use a tranquilizer?"

The man with the bandana stared back with his eyes wide open.

The driver dropped down to his knees again and ran his hands over vast rough skin before putting an ear to the elephant's chest. After a minute or so he turned around. "She's not breathing. There's no heartbeat."

The shooter looked upset. "It was a mistake. It happened too fast. I should have been more careful. We're meant to be protecting the animals, not killing them." He walked up to the lifeless body and knelt by it. "But it was an accident!" He looked around as if defending himself.

Rather than anger, a jubilant voice rose from the onlookers. "The elephant is dead!" The cry was followed by cheers. A chant began. "Kisasi! Kisasi! Kisasi!" Revenge.

TWENTY-SEVEN

But I didn't want revenge. I wanted Momma. I wanted Shaba.

It was just like when Baba died and I kept wishing that I could do anything, anything at all, to make it not true. It took a long time for my mind to believe what had happened. It was the same way now.

My eyes searched the distance, and I spotted a tiny gray blob against a tree. Mbegu had retreated but not far. Her eyes were on her mother, and she was swaying back and forth, confused and agitated. I wanted to run to her, but I couldn't move.

The KWS workers jumped into the Land Rover, and

when I heard the engine turn over, I found my strength. The car started to pull away...carrying my mother. I bolted up and ran after it, stumbling and falling and then running again.

Busara Kandenge and the other women chased after me.

"Jama! Jama!" they shouted. I felt as if a big red ball of fire was burning hot in my head. It was blinding. I tripped and crashed to the ground, my knees slamming into the rocky earth. It must have been painful, but I didn't feel anything. I was numb. I didn't have the energy to get up again.

The women caught up with me and, panting heavily, helped me up. They led me back to the manyatta, Busara Kandenge on one side and Momma's other friend Akini on the other. The rest of the women walked behind us slowly, sniffling, a wail escaping one of them now and again. They each took turns speaking.

"Jama, don't worry."

"We are here for you."

"Your mother is at peace."

"We will make a home for you."

"We understand your pain."

But their words didn't help. Because they didn't

understand. How could they? Baba was gone for good and now Momma, too. The only one who could feel the pain I felt was Mbegu, because she had also lost a mother.

I thought of her, all by herself by the river, and wondered where she would go now. I wondered if she felt as lost and alone as I did. She must.

But mostly, as we walked, I cursed myself over and over. *Why did I run? I should have stayed still as Momma told me.* If I had stayed put, Shaba wouldn't have charged, and Momma would be alive. Shaba would be, too, because there would have been no reason to shoot her. It was clear both of them were dead because of me.

I'm so sorry for not keeping still; please forgive me for not following your instructions, I spoke to Momma in my head.

After Baba died, Momma told me he watched over us. I hoped Momma could see and hear me and that she would forgive me. Something occurred to me in that moment that brought me the tiniest bit of comfort, flimsy as a reed. Maybe Momma was now with Baba somewhere.

Most Maasai do not believe in an afterlife, but I couldn't help imagining my momma and baba floating in the clouds, holding hands and looking down on me, together again.

TWENTY-EIGHT

That morning when Momma and I left to go to the river, I never imagined *this*. I would never in my worst nightmare have imagined that I would return a few hours later without her.

By the time we got to our enkajijik—or rather my enkajijik, as Momma was no longer there to share it with me—sympathizers had already gathered there.

Kokoo Naserian had abandoned her walking stick and, with her hands clasped to her chest, was slowly pacing around the yard, her chickens squawking in distress behind her as she muttered, "Why Aluna? Why not me? Why Aluna? Why not me?"

Busara Kandenge insisted I lie down, and she and the other women tiptoed around me, preparing tea. When it was ready, Busara Kandenge held the cup to my mouth. She insisted I drink all the sweet milky liquid. I didn't have the energy to fight her.

After a while I closed my eyes and pretended to sleep so that I could be left alone. The women had agreed to take turns staying with me so that I was protected, but there was really nothing they could do for me.

I kept asking myself if Momma was really gone or if I was dreaming. Would I wake up and find her cooking or sewing or pairing up sandals and packing them ready for the market in Nairobi?

But the pain inside me, which felt as if someone was drilling a hole in my heart, reminded me that I wasn't dreaming. There was no Momma to sit with and talk about Baba. I would no longer see the shy smile she had whenever we spoke about him. I would never again feel her rough, warm hands like I felt them as she rouged my face for the Eunoto ceremony.

Momma had been in such a good mood that night.

How I wished I had stayed up and spoken with her when she got home, but horrible me pretended to be asleep. If I had known then that Momma would be gone forever just a few weeks later, I would have stayed up and talked with her all night. But I didn't, and she was gone and there was absolutely nothing I could do about it.

The women sat outside, remembering Momma, and their voices floated around me.

"She was so generous, so nurturing."

"She had such a beautiful soul."

"She made the most delicious ugali stew."

Then the subject turned to what would happen to me. I listened as they spoke in hushed voices, deciding my fate.

"Kokoo Naserian is too old to raise a child," a voice said.

"Busara Kandenge has too many children of her own," added a second voice.

"And co-wives to deal with," a third voice whispered. The others chuckled.

Even in grief, they managed to gossip. Busara Kandenge must have stepped away.

"But it's just until she's ready for marriage," the second voice spoke again. I was sure it was Akini.

"The question is, Will she ever be ready for marriage? She's not like the other girls," another woman said.

Akini spoke again, "Perhaps Nadira's mother can help? But maybe not. Her husband is cruel enough to his own children—he will not manage Jama."

"Who can manage Jama?" someone asked, and there was no response.

A heavy silence fell upon the women.

In the dark, I lay still, so exhausted that my bones felt like they were made of rubber. I shut my eyes against the sounds and images in my head. The loud boom of Shaba's massive feet pounding the earth as she approached and Momma's cry as the elephant knocked her to the ground played in my ears over and over again. I shook my head to get rid of the sounds, but they stayed, got louder.

The women outside continued chatting, but I tuned them out, staring at the ceiling.

Then the horns blared. A village meeting. This time I knew exactly what it was about.

TWENTY-NINE

Busara Kandenge was back, poking her head through the doorway.

"Jama, are you awake?"

I was able to nod, barely.

"The laibon would like to host a memorial for our dear Aluna. Let's get you dressed."

I let the women lead me to the village center. The laibon stood on a robust, aged tree stump; his long robes covered most of his slender frame. Everyone gathered with their kerosene lanterns to light the night and their somber faces.

They looked at me cautiously, as if I were mad or

dangerous, as if they expected me to suddenly turn into a monster and gobble them all up. I was ushered to the front, where I sat on cushions made of lion skin. Someone draped a black veil over my shoulders.

Nadira came up and silently sat next to me, holding my hand in hers. I didn't think I had any more tears left in me, but I was so grateful to see my friend then that they started raining down my face. Nadira reached up to wipe them off, but it was a lost cause; they kept coming.

She leaned over and whispered, "Kuwa *hodari*, Jama." Be strong.

I was trying.

A hush fell on the crowd as the laibon began to speak.

"We're gathered here tonight to mourn the sudden loss of our Aluna Anyango, mother of Jama Anyango. Aluna has been a beloved member of our community since she was born thirty-two seasons ago and will be remembered with nothing but love and joy. When we think of Aluna, let us think of the comfort and laughter she spread throughout her life, rather than the tragedy that cut it short."

I heard muffled crying among the crowd. Busara Kandenge and Kokoo Naserian wept quietly. But my cheeks were now dry. I wondered if the people were judging me, wondering why Aluna's daughter was not crying.

"We need to avenge Aluna's death!" somebody called. The voice was male and agitated. Other male voices in the crowd cheered their approval.

But revenge would not bring Momma back. And besides, Shaba was already dead. An eye for an eye. A mother for a mother. What more could they want?

As if he'd heard my thoughts, the laibon reminded the gatherers that the scales were balanced because the elephant that killed Momma was already dead.

Still, the chants continued. "Kisasi! Kisasi!"

I gazed around at all the people. I knew they meant well, but it was too much. I was overwhelmed by the anger and grief and all the eyes staring at me. I realized I was searching the crowd for Momma's face, but my gaze settled on someone else.

A solemn Leku raised his hand to wave at me.

I was happy that his father was nowhere in sight. It was my fault that I didn't listen to Momma when she told me to stand still when Shaba charged, but this was Solo Mungu's fault, too. If the poacher hadn't killed an elephant from the herd, they wouldn't have even been down by the river, and they wouldn't have been upset and agitated. None of this would have happened. Momma would still be alive.

The anger that I felt realizing this bubbled in me like boiling water. A fire blazed in my head. It felt as if I were going to explode. For a second, I wished Solo Mungu were there after all, so I could shout at him, so I could tell everyone gathered here what he'd done. But I didn't.

I imagined Momma looking down on me from the sky with a frown and saying, *Jama, don't you dare raise your voice to adults.* So I kept quiet, but the anger inside me boiled so viciously my body shook.

Busara Kandenge mistook my shaking for grief. She rubbed my back to comfort me. Eventually the laibon brought the crowd under control.

"Silence!" he ordered. "This is not the time to talk about revenge and the elephants. We have gathered to mourn Aluna, a woman who meant so much to our community and whose passing will be felt by every single one of us here."

Unintelligible mumbles escaped a few mouths.

"Jama." The laibon drew the crowd's attention back to me. "Is there anything you'd like to say in honor of your mother's life?"

Everybody looked at me, a sea of solemn, dark faces and expectant eyes.

But I had no words, no voice; I had nothing.

THIRTY

When we got home from the memorial gathering, Kokoo Naserian bumbled around, feeling her way in the dark, to heat the kettle and make me tea.

I didn't want her to go to the trouble, even more so when she handed me the cup and I took a whiff of the muddy brown liquid. It smelled like swamp water and animal dung. I was grateful she couldn't see the disgusted look on my face, but she must have sensed my hesitation.

"You must drink, Jama. It will help you sleep."

There was no way I wasn't going to obey her. I

finished the whole cup, not even caring that it was burning my tongue. The pain felt good.

Kokoo Naserian kept her eyes on me, cloudy with cataracts, like even if she couldn't see me clearly, the force of her gaze was the only thing holding me together and I was going to break if she looked away. After taking my cup, she tucked me under a blanket, just like Momma used to do when I was a child. She even kissed my forehead, her lips like moth wings against my skin.

"Good night, dear."

I did not think sleep would come, and I was afraid of the nightmares it would bring, but I quickly drifted off into a dreamless void. So I was very confused to be awakened by a loud whisper.

"Jama! Jama!"

It was barely light outside, and I could hear Kokoo Naserian's cock crowing. But I was so groggy, it was hard to shake the cotton from my head. Surely I was imagining that Leku was here, calling through the mesh window. I blinked twice and rubbed my eyes and he was still there.

"Jama, you must come quick."

He must have squeezed through the opening in the fence behind the manyatta to avoid being seen by the women outside.

"They have your elephant! She isn't safe. You must come!"

Hearing this was like being splashed with ice-cold water—I was instantly alert.

"I'm coming." I sprang off the mat and out the door, where I grabbed the first pair of shoes, which happened to be Leku's blue sandals.

"Where is she?" I asked Leku, who was already a few steps ahead of me. He had on oversized brown shoes with the laces tied around his ankles to prevent their falling off. For a minute I felt guilty for wearing his sandals, but I had other pressing matters on my mind.

"The school," he said. "They found her collapsed there!"

I couldn't work out how Mbegu got to the school. She must have stumbled onto the path from the river, lost and alone, and wandered into town. I couldn't even imagine how scared she was. Actually, I could.

He went on. "She is hurt badly. Some of the villagers have gone berserk. They have been throwing stones at her, calling for revenge."

"It's not the elephants' fault! My mother died because of poachers. If they hadn't come and scared the herd, Momma would be here today." I didn't add *because of your father*, because now was not the time. "I'm not going to let anything happen to Mbegu because she has done nothing wrong. She's a poor innocent baby without a mother." I started running even faster.

He slowed down. "Well, it's an elephant, Jama. And it *was* an elephant that killed your mom, don't forget. I knew you cared, but...it's like you care about them more than your own mother."

His words hit me in the gut.

I spun around and lashed out with the full force of the back of my hand. I almost caught him in the face. But he was quick. He caught my hand, and we stood facing each other.

"Don't you ever question my love for Momma, you stupid hippo!" I was taller than him and glared down into his face. "Look at you! 'My father is a good man,'" I mimicked him in a squeaky voice. "At least my mother was a good person and my baba, too. Your father is a bad man. I know that for a fact." So much for not mentioning that.

I could see in Leku's face that my words hit him as hard as his had me. The anger in his face turned to defeat, and I felt a quick pang of regret for my ugly statement.

But I didn't have any more time to waste; Mbegu was in trouble. I shoved Leku away and sprinted toward the school.

THIRTY-ONE

The scene was worse than I could have ever imagined. As I approached, I saw a crowd of people huddled together, chanting for revenge. "Kisasi! Kisasi! Kisasi!" I recognized the men who had shouted at Momma's memorial. They were throwing spears and stones at a gray heap, cornered against a wall.

"Stop! Stop it!" I screamed, and pushed through the crowd to where Mbegu was kneeling on the ground.

I gasped at the sight of her. She was covered in bruises and dents, pockets of her flesh pulled off in chunks, streaks of blood all over her limp body. I saw that her heavy chest struggled to take in air, and I feared that if one more stone hit her, she would die.

Without a second thought, I threw my body over hers.

The men jeered at me, but I didn't care. I wrapped my body around Mbegu gently enough to keep my weight off her. They wouldn't be able to hurt her with my body as a shield.

"What are you doing?" several voices called out. "Get up or you'll get hurt!"

"I'm not getting up!" I was so angry with them that I raised my voice. "If you want to hurt her, you'll have to hurt me, too."

"Don't be an idiot," I heard someone say. "This elephant's mother killed *your* mother, killed *our* Aluna. What's wrong with you?"

I didn't budge. I was getting immune to the accusation that I didn't love Momma. Or that I loved her less than Mbegu.

The crowd continued to shout at me to move. They hurled insults.

"Heartless!"

"Coward!"

"Embarrassment!"

But I stayed put. Even when a rock aimed at Mbegu struck my cheek and cut it open, I didn't move. I didn't even raise my hand to stop the trickle of blood that ran down my face.

"That's Aluna's daughter!" a female voice shouted. "Control yourselves!" It was Busara Kandenge. "Are you out of your minds?" she asked, her voice trembling.

Someone called out that I was creating the problem for myself. "Get her out of here!" they yelled.

As Busara Kandenge argued on my behalf and pleaded with me to get up, I remained with my arms draped over Mbegu's rough torso and my face resting against the prickly bristles on her neck. The loud voices merged and faded around me. I couldn't make out what was being said anymore and I didn't care. These people were all traitors and hypocrites. They watched me grow up and loved Momma, but were willing to harm me just to avenge her death. It didn't make sense; nothing made sense.

I felt Mbegu's skin grow cold and her body begin to shake. Then I realized that it was me. I was the one shaking. Cold sweat trickled down my back.

It hit me all over again, harder than the stone had: *My momma is dead. I am alone in the world.* But then I heard the faint thrumming of Mbegu's heart beneath my ear and I remembered I wasn't alone. I had Mbegu and I was going to save her.

THIRTY-TWO

I

s that Jama Anyango?"

The question came from somewhere above me; it was deep and raspy and steeped in sadness. I peered up and saw Laibon Umoja's tall, thin frame draped in his red-and-blue-checked robe standing over me.

"Enkai tadamuiyook," he sighed. God have mercy. He closed his eyes, then turned to the angry crowd. "Look what you've done to her." He stared at the cut in my cheek, from which a few drops of blood had dripped onto my shirt. His voice was low and calm, but from the stern look on his face and the tremor in his voice it was obvious he was angry.

"But, Laibon, she won't leave the elephant's side—we had no choice!" A man in the crowd stepped forward to explain the situation. He was short and carried a spear taller than he was. "We have other things to do today! Get her out of the way, we kill the elephant, and we go," he said, swinging the spear around.

Heads in the crowd bobbed in approval.

"Hold your stones," the laibon ordered. His extra-long arms and legs jutted out in different directions as he crouched over me.

"My dear Jama," he spoke slowly. "Do not put yourself in harm's way. You and I might not think it necessary. However, these men are following the teachings of our ancestors, who believed that as long as justice among earth's creatures was off-kilter, the universe would be out of balance. Unless an eye was taken for an eye, the scales of good and evil would always be tilted toward evil."

"But Shaba is already dead!" I said, my teeth chattering from cold and fear and grief. "You said the scales are balanced!"

"Who is Shaba?" the laibon asked, confused.

I felt childish for giving the elephants names, for thinking they were my friends, but it was still the truth.

"That's the elephant who killed Momma. This is her baby."

THIRTY-THREE

The laibon looked over the pitiful creature under me. "This elephant does not look like it will survive anyway. Let the people be done here, and you can go home and grieve for your mother."

"But, Laibon, I know Momma would not want an innocent elephant to die."

"The elephants are not innocent!" the man with the long spear screamed. "Did you not witness the herd attack your mother? You could have died, too!"

Leku came closer and squatted down to eye level. It was then I noticed a deep purple bruise on his neck. I could imagine just where—or rather who—it came from.

Momma had once told me that people who were treated cruelly tended to be cruel to others because cruelty was all they knew. It explained why Leku was horrible to everyone, and I felt a wave of pity for him.

He shook his head at me slowly. "Jama, just let this go."

I felt my courage ebbing away, replaced with a hopelessness. Then Mbegu shuddered under me and struggled to take a breath, and I came back to my senses. She was innocent. Momma would not agree to an elephant being killed to avenge her death.

"It's the poachers that killed Momma," I heard myself shout. "It's Solo Mungu's fault. He let the poachers come!"

As soon as the words escaped my lips, the crowd gasped, then fell silent. Slowly, murmurs arose as my accusation sank in.

"It's true. I saw him giving money—"

"Enough, child!" The laibon looked at me, impatience flashing in his eyes.

The crowd started up again. "You see, she's a problem child. Poor Aluna, what did she do to deserve such a disrespectful child?" The woman's voice was followed by a chorus of clucking and *tsk-tsk*ing in agreement.

The laibon clapped twice and two men stepped forward. "Take this child to my manyatta," he commanded. "Tell them to clean her up and feed her. I will come and meditate with her later."

I lashed out with my arms and legs, but the men gripped me with iron-strong hands and yanked me off Mbegu.

I screamed as the crowd started to move in on her, then I realized the roar in my ears was not in my mind but the sound of a Land Rover roaring to a halt. It was the same two men from the river yesterday, from the Kenya Wildlife Service.

"We have a situation," the driver spoke into a walkie-talkie as he surveyed the scene, his eyes bulging with alarm. "Request for backup," he said, hopping out of the jeep. His partner went and stood in front of the vehicle, tranquilizer gun raised and ready. Today he had traded a green bandana for a black one.

"What the hell is going on here?" The man with the gun directed his question to the laibon.

"We have a situation, and I am dealing with it," the laibon responded calmly.

"Release the girl," the officer ordered.

The men dropped me, and I scrambled back to my

place beside Mbegu. My body hurt, but I didn't wince because I wanted to appear strong and fearless. Like someone nobody should dare mess with.

"You have no jurisdiction over my people," Laibon Umoja reminded the officers. "You don't have any jurisdiction on our land."

Both men stood their ground. "With all due respect, sir, we may not have jurisdiction over you or your people, but it's our duty to protect the wildlife of the national parks, especially the endangered species."

"And you have a baby elephant imprisoned," said the bandanaed man, gripping his gun tightly. "Look what you've done to her! You're killing her."

"Justice must be served!" someone said, and a rock whistled through the air and struck Mbegu's wilted ear. She let out a weak whimper.

"Step back!" One of the officers pointed their tranquilizer gun at the crowd. "The next person to throw anything gets shot. This is a warning. Back away!"

THIRTY-FOUR

There was a standoff, guns pointed, rocks poised, the crowd outnumbering the KWS staff tenfold. I wondered how long it would last and how it would end.

Mbegu's heart rate was slowing; her time was running out. It was up to me to do something. I wasn't going to let Mbegu die like Momma and Shaba. I had to help her, but how?

Lying over Mbegu wasn't enough to save her. I realized I had to think fast.

Then, on the dusty horizon, I saw a dark green truck approaching. When it was close enough, I was able to make out the Naibunga Conservancy logo stenciled on the hood; a black antelope within a ring.

My only hope was that whoever was in that truck could help.

But the Land Rover stopped in the distance. My heart stopped as well. Why didn't they come closer? Couldn't they see us?

Time was running out. I wasn't sure what to do. If I moved away from Mbegu, the crowd would stone her to death. If I stayed put, she would still die without medical attention.

In a flash, I made up my mind. I counted to ten and sprang to my feet. "Don't let them hurt her!" I yelled at the KWS workers.

And I was off. Running, sprinting, leaving all the bewildered, unfinished questions—*Where? Why? What?*—in the dust. I tuned out the curses being flung at me and kept running. I prayed that the two men would keep the crowd at bay just a little longer. I prayed that Mbegu could hold out just a little while longer.

"Over here!" I waved my arms at the Naibunga Conservancy Land Rover. "Here! Help me! I need your help!"

The driver sped toward me and then slammed on the brakes, sending a spray of dirt in the air. "What's happening?"

"An elephant," I heaved. My lungs felt as if they were on fire. "In trouble. Revenge. They hurt her," I explained between gasps. I hoped I was making sense.

"Whoa, whoa," the man said. "Slow down." He was wearing a uniform, a green jumpsuit with matching canvas belt and beret. His name tag read WARDEN, NAI-BUNGA CONSERVANCY.

"No time," I heaved. "She's dying. The baby elephant."

"Get in." He reached across the passenger seat and opened the door for me. "Let's go."

THIRTY-FIVE

I jumped into the car and we barreled the short distance back to the schoolyard. As he drove, I tried to tell him as much as possible about the past few days. I rambled on about Mbegu and Momma being trampled, and the dead mother elephant.

"My name is Ojwang; what is your name?" he asked.

"I'm Jama."

"Okay, Jama," he said, putting his hand on my shoulder. "We are going to take care of this."

I was so relieved to hear him say *we*. It felt good to

have a partner; someone other than me wanted to save Mbegu.

Soon we got back to the scene.

"Everybody back away from the elephant or I'll shoot!" Ojwang jumped out of the Land Rover and pointed his rifle at the crowd.

They stumbled back, fear on their faces. I hoped they would give up and scatter away, but they stayed put.

Ojwang hurried over to Mbegu and grimaced. For a second, he looked sad, then he quickly readopted his serious expression.

"Wamai," Ojwang addressed the KWS worker with the black bandana. "Put down your tranquilizer and take this," he said, handing him his rifle.

Ojwang crouched down and felt for Mbegu's heartbeat. He then whispered something to her, and her eyes flickered open.

I watched with astonishment as he slipped one arm through the crevasses of both Mbegu's armpits and helped her up so that she was standing on trembling legs.

"Jama, help," Ojwang said. "The door..." He nodded toward the front door of the school, painted a navy blue. "Open it."

I rushed to the door and thanked Enkai that it

was unlocked. Ojwang then coaxed feeble Mbegu one step at a time into the classroom. I could tell that she knew he was on her side because she lumbered instinctively toward him. I followed closely behind and once we were safely inside, I slammed the door shut behind us and locked it. I barricaded it with a chair for good measure before I turned to Ojwang and said excitedly, "Look, she's standing!" But just then, Mbegu's knees buckled and she collapsed like a rag doll.

"Is she dead?" I asked Ojwang.

"No, but she will be if we don't get the DSWT in here immediately."

I didn't have time to ask what he meant. A rock clattered against the door, followed by the sharp, metallic-sounding airburst of a tranquilizer dart leaving the barrel. So different from the sound from when Shaba was shot. A man hollered in shock, which was followed by a thump. I winced at the sound. The image of Shaba falling heavily to the ground flashed through my mind. My eyes shot to the barricaded door, and I hoped it was sturdy enough to keep us safe.

Ojwang produced a flip phone from his pocket and dialed fast. He spoke in rushed tones to whoever was on the other end of the line and then snapped his phone shut.

"They're on their way," Ojwang said, resting one hand on Mbegu's chest. "Her heartbeat is slow but within safe range." He seemed to be talking to himself more than to me.

"Who's on their way?" I asked.

"DSWT. The David Sheldrick Wildlife Trust. It's a sort of hospital and nursery for animals. They specialize in taking care of orphaned elephants. A team is flying in from Nairobi," Ojwang said, glancing at his wristwatch.

"Nairobi? That's far."

"They should be here in about forty-five minutes. Let's hope she can hang on until then. We don't have any other options. Only they can save her."

THIRTY-SIX

I sat in a corner with my knees folded up to my chest, feeling helpless. I tried to imagine Wamai with the rifle pointed confidently at the crowd and them knowing that they ought to take him seriously.

I glanced nervously at the four small windows that lined the walls on either side of the room, covered in smudged glass. Even if anyone could break the glass, the windows were too narrow for an adult to maneuver through. At least that's what I tried to convince myself. I tried to have confidence in the chair as a barricade, confidence that if anybody lunged for the door, Wamai would stop them. I tried to reassure myself that

Mbegu's wounds looked much worse than they actually were. But the harder I tried to quiet the panic, the louder it got.

After a while I stood up and started pacing back and forth around the classroom. It was such a strange sight, all our wooden desks lined up in five neat rows—mine right in the front—and the chalkboard and the artwork on the walls, and then a sick baby elephant on the floor.

I kept glancing at the clock. It made me think of the first day I met Mbegu, when I was so restless in this very classroom and the clock hands weren't moving fast enough. Just as they weren't now. After a period of pacing, I went back and collapsed next to Mbegu, watching her shallow breaths. I let my mind go to the worst-case scenario. *If Mbegu dies, and Ojwang drives away and the KWS team leaves, what will become of me? Everyone will have turned on me.*

"They're here." Ojwang's words cut into my thoughts. Or was it my dreams? I found myself sitting on the floor in a daze. I sat up, blinking and disoriented. I must have dozed off.

"Stay here and keep an eye on Mbegu. Make sure she keeps breathing," Ojwang said and dashed out.

I hurriedly barricaded the door again. I heard him instructing one of the KWS officers to take his Land Rover and pick up the DSWT team from where their plane had landed.

After the car drove off there was silence. I was watching Mbegu's chest rise and fall. She was still breathing, but I wasn't sure what I would do if she stopped. All I could do to keep her alive was pray to Enkai and hope that would be enough.

I crept to the door to peek through a crack and check on the scene outside. Ojwang and the KWS backup team had their rifles aimed, and the crowd was keeping their distance, looking to the laibon for guidance, muttering among themselves.

When Mbegu let out a feeble cough, followed by a whimper, I rushed back to her.

"I'm sorry, I'm sorry," I whispered.

She lifted her trunk ever so slightly, and I could tell that she knew my voice. When I leaned closer to her, she tried to lift it again, as if to nuzzle me.

"No, Mbegu, don't. Save your strength. I'm here for you. I'm not leaving you, okay?"

Drops of wetness appeared on Mbegu's skin. My tears.

I could tell my voice comforted her, so I kept talking. I told her that I was sorry about her mother and the other elephant in the herd that was slaughtered. It hurt me that I still didn't know who it was. I told her about my mother and how she was gone.

"We're orphans now, Mbegu." Saying it out loud made it real. Again I wondered what would happen to us, Mbegu and me.

THIRTY-SEVEN

I t felt as though hours had passed by the time the Land Rover pulled up. I heard the rescue team jumping out, slamming doors behind them.

"Who are these people?" I heard more than one voice from the crowd ask.

"This is our property," the laibon said. "Who are these men? They are not welcome."

I didn't hear Ojwang reply, but seconds later he was knocking on the door. "Jama, open up!"

I rushed to move the chair away and let them in. Behind him a team of two men and one woman filed in holding duffel bags. They wore green coats and black boots, and moved swiftly. I backed away as they unfolded a heavy black canvas sheet and, with their combined strength, rolled Mbegu onto it. They talked among themselves, very rapidly, using medical terms I didn't understand.

They quickly examined Mbegu's wounds, assessing the damage and danger. One man produced a bottle of milk from his duffel bag and placed it at Mbegu's dry lips. With a gloved hand, he tilted her heavy head so that the milk trickled into her mouth.

"I thought they can only drink their mother's milk," I whispered to Ojwang.

"It's a special milk for baby elephants made by the DSWT," Ojwang whispered back.

My heart dropped when I saw the special milk dribble back out of Mbegu's mouth.

"She's not drinking it," one of the men stated the obvious. "Her body's in too much shock."

"Too much trauma," the other agreed. "We've got to get her back to the Trust if there's any hope."

A decision was made, and everyone started acting in concert. They each held on to a side of the heavy black canvas cloth where Mbegu lay and, on the count of three, they hoisted her up. I opened the door for them.

THIRTY-EIGHT

Where are you taking the elephant?" a voice from the crowd asked. It had been almost two hours now, but there were still a dozen or so people gathered outside. The pointed guns kept them at a safe distance, but their outrage reignited at the sight of Mbegu being carried away. Their yelling resumed.

"She is our property; you can't take her from us!"

"You don't have the right!"

"Leave us alone!"

The laibon stepped into the path of our group. "Where are you taking the elephant? Who do you think you are? Coming onto our property and taking our wildlife?"

"Your wildlife? But you were about to kill her— remember?" Ojwang sounded and looked irritated. He took his rifle back from Wamai.

"If you carry her one more step, we'll attack! You'll leave us no choice," said the man with the spear, who appeared to have appointed himself spokesperson.

"Try," Ojwang challenged him. "This is a real gun, my friend."

The crowd exchanged wary glances and suddenly seemed hesitant except for a few men.

"He wouldn't dare shoot us," the spokesman said.

"Try me. I *will* shoot," Ojwang said, his nose flaring with anger.

Either the man didn't believe Ojwang or his ego wouldn't let him back down. He tried to save face. "Habu tuende," he called, gesturing to the few men around to join him as he stepped forward defiantly.

I held my breath.

"Wait!" a member of the rescue team called out. "Before you act, think carefully. The consequences of harming an endangered species are severe. Even wounding an endangered animal has a fine. If you let us go now, we won't have you arrested for harming the baby elephant. Understand?"

"You think you can scare us with threats? Tell us, what are the consequences for the elephant for killing a human being? Our Aluna is dead," the self-appointed spokesperson said. "Fine us? We will also fine you for killing our Aluna."

Dread climbed its way up my spine. I worried that the time spent talking to the men meant less time to save Mbegu.

Ojwang must have been thinking the same thing. "Let's get her out of here," he said under his breath.

They carried Mbegu to the truck. As soon as they laid her down, the team started to buckle her in, and Ojwang walked back up to the crowd, which continued to close in.

THIRTY-NINE

Y ou think I won't shoot?" Ojwang shouted. "You dare me?"

BANG! It came from nowhere.

I dropped to my knees and looked around. Ojwang was still holding the weapon up in the air, where he'd shot. A warning.

It worked. The men scattered, falling over one another.

Ojwang turned around and walked back to the car smiling triumphantly. The KWS men followed him. "Sorry, guys," Ojwang said to the rescue team. "But that is the only language they understand."

"You could have at least warned us!" One of the rescuers glared at Ojwang, who didn't take any notice. He seemed pleased with himself for having frightened the man with the spear and his followers. As the team settled in the car, the crowd reassembled at a farther distance. Ojwang walked around the car and jumped into the driver's seat.

"Jama, come, let's go home." Busara Kandenge had pushed to the front of the crowd and was by my side.

"She's not welcome here anymore!" It was the man with the spear.

"Does the land belong to you?" Busara Kandenge shouted angrily. "Were Aluna and Hamadi not of this land?"

"She's a traitor!" came another voice.

"You talk about honoring Aluna, but you shun her daughter?"

"She's an embarrassment and a curse to our community."

Ojwang heard the venom in their voices and turned to me. "Jama, are you okay?" he asked.

"I don't know," I said, my legs quivering. I wasn't sure if they were shaking out of fear of my community or fear that I would never see Mbegu again. Ojwang hopped out of the Land Rover and walked over to me, his rifle firmly by his side.

"There's room for you in the car," he said. "You can come with us."

"No!" Busara Kandenge said. "She has family here."

That wasn't exactly true. I had my great-great-aunt Kokoo Naserian, I suppose.

I thought about how if I got into this car, I wouldn't be able to say goodbye. I pictured her now, hobbling out to feed the chickens, worrying about what would happen to me. There would be no one to listen to her stories.

"She can go!" another voice shouted to more cheers.

"You are all shameless!" Busara Kandenge shouted back.

From behind her a shadow appeared and then Leku stepped forward. He didn't say any words, but there was a nod, barely there, when Busara turned to me and said, "Please don't go, Jama."

Was it possible that Leku cared if I stayed? Would we actually become friends if I remained? For a fleeting second, I imagined going on long walks with him down to the river and sitting with him under my favorite tree. But then someone else in the crowd shouted, and like that, the bubble was burst.

I took a deep breath and squared my shoulders. "They don't want me here, Momma Busara. Momma is gone. No one wants me," I said, and the words sent a throbbing pain through my chest. Every time I mentioned Momma or thought of her, it was like someone was stabbing me right in my heart.

I turned over the few options I had in my mind. They weren't very promising. In fact, they didn't look like options at all, just shreds of minor pros and dreadful cons.

"Is this true?" Busara turned to the laibon, who had come closer. "Is there no home for this child?"

He ignored her and waved a clenched fist at Ojwang. "How dare you shoot at us? First thing tomorrow, I will come to your offices and report you." The laibon's voice shook with anger.

"Go ahead," Ojwang said, then turned to me. "Jama, we have to leave—the elephant can't wait."

I couldn't think about it any longer. Mbegu was running out of time. I was also scared that the situation was getting out of hand because everyone was getting angrier. Even Ojwang was losing his cool.

I took another deep breath and made a decision, knowing it would change my life forever.

"I'm coming with you."

We had to get out fast.

"I'm sorry, Momma Busara. I'm so sorry," I said, although I was not sure what I was apologizing for.

"But what will happen to you? Where are you going?" she asked, her voice sad and low such that no one else could hear her.

"I don't know." It was a terrifying fact. "Will you please tell Kokoo Naserian goodbye for me?"

I turned slightly to look at Leku and waved a hand.

With that, I walked away and didn't look back at her or Leku, whom I sensed watching me. I couldn't bring myself to do it.

I climbed into the back of the Land Rover, where the seats had been folded down to make space for Mbegu. I rested my head on her back and tried not to think about what would happen next, where I was going, or what waited for me when I got there.

FORTY

The tiny airplane swayed and bucked as it climbed into the air. Flying didn't feel as smooth and free as I imagined it would whenever I watched planes up in the sky.

Momma used to say to me, "Be careful what you wish for, Jama. Some wishes are best staying just that." She was right.

I had always wished I could fly like a bird, but as I sat gripping the seat and watching the darkening clouds float past through the small window, I changed my mind. The plane rattled and bounced around wildly, like a leaf in the wind, sending my brain wobbling inside my head. When the plane dipped, my stomach felt as if it was going to jump out of my mouth. The engine roared like a wild animal, vibrating deep in my eardrums.

Minutes ago, Ojwang had helped me onto the plane before saying goodbye. I was surprised at how upset I was that he was leaving, or rather that he was staying put and we were leaving him at the airfield.

"I need to stay here, calm things down. The preserve is my office." He smiled at me. "I will keep the elephants safe, Jama. You have my word."

I cursed myself that on the ride to the airport I was too distracted worrying about Mbegu to tell him about Solo Mungu, and now there wasn't time. The DSWT team was clearly eager to close the door and take off. I threw myself into his arms for a warm hug. "Thank you for your help."

"You're a brave girl, Jama."

When he saw me hesitate to get on the plane, he gave me a reassuring smile. "You'll be fine." I think he meant on the flight, but maybe he meant when it came to everything else, too.

When I felt the plane was no longer climbing into the sky and was flying in a straight line, I let go of my grip on the armrests and looked toward where the DSWT team surrounded Mbegu.

I noticed they were each wearing name tags. The two men on the team were Matthew and Adan, and the woman was Dafina. They worked with serious faces, attaching and inserting various tubes, cords, wires, and needles into Mbegu's little body. She was hooked up to so many gadgets that she looked like the back of the computer in Miss Mutua's classroom.

One of the cords was attached to a black screen that had a horizontal blue line glowing across that moved up and down in tiny spikes and dramatic dips. From the way the team kept looking at the screen, I knew it was telling them if Mbegu was getting better or worse.

"Her heart rate is starting to stabilize," Dafina said.

We all stared as the blue line began to map a steady and even up-down pattern. It looked like a drawing of a landscape: mountain, valley, mountain, valley. I figured it out: mountain, valley, mountain, valley meant Mbegu was doing fine; a solid flat line that didn't move meant... well, I wasn't even going to think about that.

FORTY-ONE

S he hasn't been drinking the milk," said Matthew, lifting the milk bottle to Mbegu's limp, open mouth.

"But she's absorbing the IV fluids, which is a good start," said Dafina.

"She'll drink the milk, Matthew." Adan had a very soothing voice, low and slow. "Have some faith. Patience."

"Patience?" Matthew scoffed. "We don't have time to be patient. Look at—"

"Quiet," Dafina interrupted. "We *have* to be patient because there is nothing else to do, okay? And keep your voices down; the last thing we want is to upset her any more than she already is."

Reluctantly, the two men nodded in agreement and returned to checking the screen and the other instruments attached to Mbegu.

Dafina looked from Mbegu over to where I was sitting at the back of the plane, as if seeing me for the first time. Holding on to the handles on the plane's curved walls for support, she walked toward me.

She's going to kick me out. I panicked. *She's going to shove me off the back of the plane like a sack of dirt.* If there's one thing I had learned that day, it was that I was dispensable. If people who had known me all my life could banish me, what chance did I have with strangers?

But surprisingly she crouched down to my level, and I saw that she was not angry but concerned.

"Are you all right?" she asked, reaching for a blue metal box lodged in the side of the plane.

I nodded.

Dafina opened the box, pulled a damp cloth from a packet, and wiped the dried blood from the cut on my cheek.

It stung but I didn't say anything. By that point I had decided that I was going to be strong. I had to be strong for Mbegu and me. I was going to be like Leku, who acted as if he had no feelings. Maybe he was on to something; maybe it was the best way to survive. Thinking of Leku gave me the tiniest pinch in my chest.

"Are you all right?" Dafina asked again, sticking a square of gauze on my cheek. Perhaps she had not seen me nod.

"No," I said. "I mean, yes. No. I don't know. I'm sorry." I stuttered, unsure of how I felt or what to say.

"What are you sorry for?" Dafina put her hand on my knee, which I realized had been trembling despite my efforts to look strong. "Ojwang told us the danger you were in. We weren't going to leave you in that situation. What's your name?"

"Jama. My name is Jama."

"Okay." Her mouth lifted into a smile. "Well, Jama, you're safe now. I know you've been through hell and back. I'm sorry to hear about your mother." She paused, and compassion blazed from her eyes. "But just try to relax now, okay? We'll be there soon."

Dafina continued to stare at me with pity, and it felt very awkward looking back into her face because I didn't know what to say next.

Then the moment was interrupted.

FORTY-TWO

BEEP, BEEEEP, BEBEBEEEEEEEP! The monitor
started to beep frantically. Dafina jumped up
and rushed back to Mbegu.

"Her heart rate is dropping quickly," Adan said, the
alarm clear in his voice. The team formed a tight circle around Mbegu. I squirmed in my seat and peered
through a small gap between two green coats. Mbegu
was thrashing in fear, but her movements were weak
and fatigued.

"The IV should keep her stable until we land,"
Adan said.

"But it's *not*." Matthew was clearly frustrated.

"She's still breathing, but for how long? Her body is in a heightened state of trauma and panic; she can't go on much longer like this."

"Jama!"

I jumped at the mention of my name. Dafina was looking straight at me. "Jama, come quick." She beckoned me over.

I meant to hurry over, but my seat belt had other plans. It took what was probably a few seconds to unbuckle, but with Dafina waiting and watching, it seemed like ages as I tussled with the buckle before I finally freed myself. My face burning with embarrassment, I rushed to the huddle around Mbegu.

"This is Jama," Dafina announced to the team, who hadn't acknowledged me in any way. "Ojwang told me she kept the calf calm back in the classroom. The elephant knows and trusts her."

"Is she trained?" Adan asked.

"Trained?" Dafina asked, raising an impatient eyebrow. "In the *comforting of elephants*? No."

"Does she know what she's doing?" Matthew asked as if I weren't standing a foot away. He and Adan were suddenly on the same side. "Another person crowding around will just get in the way. She's just a child."

But I wasn't a child. I stopped being one when Baba died, and now Momma was gone, too. It's hard to be a child when you don't have parents. I may have liked to run and climb trees and play with the elephants. I may not have felt ready to be a wife or a mother anytime soon. But after everything I'd been through, I was *not* a child, even if I wanted to be. And I did know what I was doing, with Mbegu anyway. So I pushed my way toward her, ignoring Matthew and Adan.

Before I could get to her, the heart monitor made an alarming screeching noise. Matthew took out two plastic panels with handles attached to coiling cords.

"What is that?" I asked Dafina, as I read the writing on one of the panels. AUTOMATED EXTERNAL DEFIBRILLATOR.

"She's going into cardiac arrest; her heart is stopping. That's a machine that can help get her heartbeat back to normal again. It gives her a shock." Dafina had quickly moved past the idea of me helping. From her words and the worried faces around Mbegu, I didn't think I was needed anymore, nor wanted.

Suddenly, a crackling sound came from a small speaker mounted onto one of the walls, followed by a voice. "Prepare for landing. I repeat, prepare for landing."

I was too worried about Mbegu to even be fearful that the plane was quickly diving toward the ground.

"Jama, go sit down for landing," Matthew said, and this time Dafina nodded in agreement. He knelt down with the defibrillator machine next to Mbegu.

From my seat, I had the perfect angle to look right in Mbegu's eyes. I knew she could see me, so I didn't move. Instead I kept my eyes fixed on hers. I didn't look away when Matthew curled his arms around Mbegu so that the panels could press against her chest.

"Analyzing heart rhythm," a robotic male voice spoke loudly out of the machine. "Preparing shock," it said just as the plane dropped several feet and sent my heart into my throat.

"Shock will be delivered in three, two, one," the machine said. "Delivering shock."

FORTY-THREE

I watched from my seat as an electric shock surged through Mbegu, making her whole body shake. Matthew held the panels down firmly to keep himself from being thrown off.

"Shock delivered," the machine reported, and everything went silent. We all turned to the heart monitor. The running blue line began to move, small valley, small mountain here and there, but mostly it remained flat.

I gripped my armrests tight as the plane's wheels bounced against the earth followed by an ear-piercing screech as they skidded to a halt.

"Come on, come on," Matthew muttered, his eyes darting between Mbegu and the monitor.

Mbegu, please, I prayed. *You can do it. You can make it.*

My next thought was a selfish one: *If this elephant dies, I will have nothing. No Momma, no Baba, no community, nowhere to live, nowhere to go, no one to love me.*

"Please stay alive, Mbegu, please stay alive," I heard myself whispering. "You have to. I can't lose you, too."

FORTY-FOUR

verything moved fast after the plane landed, so fast my head felt as if it were full of buzzing bees.

Mbegu was rushed to a truck that was waiting for us on the tarmac at a small airport that was little more than a concrete strip in a sea of dirt.

As we drove, the sky got darker and darker with each inch that the sun sank. With every mile, I couldn't help thinking of the growing distance between me and everything I'd ever known. And even though I knew Momma was gone forever, I still felt as though I was getting farther and farther away from her. The farthest

I'd ever ventured away from my village was the watering hole where I'd found the elephants.

I was so rarely in a car, and the ride was bumpy. I already felt woozy from being in the sky and from the drama of the day, and the combined effects convinced me that I was seconds from throwing up.

Fortunately, before that could happen Dafina announced we were close, and we turned into a driveway secured by a gate. Through the truck's headlights, I read a large sign: THE DAVID SHELDRICK WILDLIFE TRUST.

Throughout the ride, I'd kept glancing back at Mbegu, who had her eyes closed the whole time. She seemed calmer now, like she was sleeping, but I didn't know if that was better or worse. Was she just slipping away?

We pulled into a compound of small buildings, and some staff rushed out to help. As Mbegu was carried away, I followed close behind. I was scared of losing sight of her. Scared that if I didn't keep up with the team, they would forget all about me and I would get lost.

We walked into one of the buildings. On the wall by the doorway there was a drawing, a big circle around the faces of an elephant, a rhinoceros, and a man with a hat. Underneath were the words: *A lifetime dedicated to the protection and preservation of Africa's wilderness and its denizens, particularly endangered species such as elephants and black rhino.*

I knew all about the wilderness and elephants and black rhinos, but denizens? I wondered what animal it was and what it looked like.

Mbegu was rushed through a second door into a small room with a table and medical instruments and supplies, and again I trailed behind on everyone's heels. The team spoke to one another as they moved.

It was clear that Mbegu was still in grave danger.

FORTY-FIVE

atthew was carrying a breathing machine connected to the tube in Mbegu's mouth. Another team member was holding up two plastic bags of liquid that were draining into Mbegu's body. Adan carried the heart monitor.

Everyone around Mbegu seemed to be doing something except me. I had never felt so helpless. It was a feeling I hated.

The room was cold, and I shivered in my thin shirt, dotted with brown spots of dried blood. I looked down and realized I was still wearing Leku's sandals. It felt like another lifetime that I had put on these sandals, or got them in the first place. Memories of my old life—that's how I thought of it now, *old*—were like painful stabs.

I caught a glimpse of my reflection in one of the windows. With the big white bandage that Dafina had placed on my cheek, my small round head, and my eyes—which looked even bigger given how tired I was—I looked like an alien in one of the science fiction books in my school library.

"How's her breathing?" Matthew asked.

"Not good," Adan replied. "She's struggling. Hope the IV vitamins kick in soon."

"She's still too traumatized," said Dafina.

She has to drink the milk; she won't drink the milk.

Their words began to sound like a bad song stuck in a loop, fragments of sentences repeating—echoing—over and over in my head.

Her heartbeat is unstable; her heartbeat is stable for now; the oxygen isn't working; she isn't inhaling properly; she's too traumatized; she's too traumatized; she's too traumatized, she's too traumatized.

I put my hands over my ears to block it all out, but all that did was trap the voices in my head.

Matthew and the team pushed through another

door in the back of the room—it opened onto a yard enclosed by mesh with a netted ceiling. The sky was black, but a row of hanging lanterns lit up the space. When I adjusted to the dim lighting, I looked around and opened my eyes even wider when I spotted two baby rhinoceroses staring back at me through wooden slats. There was a long line of these wooden stalls.

Much to my delight, I also spotted five or six baby elephants. Through the openings between the slats, I could see that they were sleeping, covered in color-ful blankets. In the corner of each stall lay a heap of branches and leaves on the floor. A midnight snack for the babies, I guessed.

I watched as Matthew and the team laid Mbegu down in an empty stall.

Beep beeeeeeeep! Beeeeeep beep beeeeeeeeeeep! It was the dreaded sound of Mbegu's heartbeat failing again. Every face around Mbegu fell at the same time.

"She's flatlining," Matthew said grimly. "The oxy-gen isn't getting to her lungs."

Mbegu's eyes fluttered open for the briefest of sec-onds and then closed.

"What are you waiting for? Shock her!" The words just jumped out of my mouth. It took me a second to realize I had cried out. Even though Dafina had already explained to me earlier that the defibrillator hardly ever worked the second time.

The crew stopped and stared at me, in surprise and pity. A few of them even looked confused as to why a strange, scrawny girl was there yelling at them.

I didn't blame them. I would stare at me with pity, too. I knew I looked and sounded crazy, but seeing Mbegu's eyes start to close made me panic.

Just then, a different sound layered over the dreaded, erratic beeping. A sound I was familiar with from all my time with the elephants. A soft rumble.

FORTY-SIX

T he other elephants in neighboring stalls had woken up. They peered through the slats to look at Mbegu and tried to reach her with their trunks. I recognized the friendliness in their calls. They were welcoming her.

"Look." Dafina pointed at Mbegu. "Her eyes."

Mbegu's eyes opened slightly, then more fully.

"Her heart rate is stabilizing." Matthew looked at the monitor. All of us stared at it, too, watching as it slowly regained a steady pattern.

Beep . . . beep . . . beep . . . beep . . . beep . . . beep . . .

The elephants continued their calls, reaching their trunks through the slats, and Mbegu's glassy eyes stayed open. The monitor remained consistent.

"It seems...," Dafina spoke hesitantly. "It seems she's starting to breathe steadily."

"She's comforted by the other elephants," Adan said, then he spoke to me directly for the first time. "This is good, Jama. If she breathes, she can make it."

"Let's not speak too soon." Matthew kept his eyes glued to the monitor and two fingers on Mbegu's pulse. "We need to stitch up her wounds while she's sedated."

I watched the monitor nervously as the medical instruments were pulled from a big metal box and the crew got to work on the cuts and bruises all over Mbegu's body.

The glowing blue line was steady, but every jump up or down felt like a punch to my stomach. I took a deep breath and pretended that I was in control of the line, that I had the power to keep it even, that as long as I was conducting the pattern of beeps, Mbegu would be just fine.

The sounds of elephants softly bellowing and scissors snipping and medical tools tapping delicately against a tray all fell away, and all that was left in the world was Mbegu and me and the blue line and the steady *beep...beep...beep.*

"Can I?" I asked Matthew, nodding to Mbegu. I wanted to touch her again, to be close to her.

"Sure."

I knelt by Mbegu's head and rubbed her trunk. I knew the cleaning and stitching of her wounds probably hurt. I remember Momma rubbing my scrapes with ointment made from the bark of an olchilishili tree and the sharp sting of it. But Mbegu was being very strong because she was a fighter. Her big round eyes focused on me like she was telling me not to let go. And I didn't. Not until Matthew was done with the very last stitch. Her body was a patchwork of purple bruises and white splotches where medicine covered the wounds. It was good to see her without a tube down her throat, at least.

"Her breathing remains excellent," Dafina said.

"Let's try the milk," said Matthew. He lifted a bottle with a bright orange nozzle—it looked exactly like a baby bottle, only five times larger. He tilted it to Mbegu's mouth, and she latched on.

"She's drinking!" Dafina exclaimed.

We all watched with a mix of glee and pride at Mbegu sucking hungrily on her bottle.

I wanted to ask if she was going to be okay, but the words didn't come out of my mouth. Instead, as soon as I stood up, a white cloud descended on me like I was floating into space. I rocked on my feet trying to steady myself. Everything around me became still.

And then I heard it, Momma's voice, like she was right next to me: *You did it, Jama. You saved her. I'm so proud of you.*

I looked around to see where the voice came from, but everything was spinning round and round, faster and faster until there was only darkness.

FORTY-SEVEN

When I woke up, I was in a bed with a plaid flannel blanket draped over me, and covered head to toe in a slick film of sweat. The ceiling was uncomfortably low, way too close to my face. There was a wooden barricade around the bed, trapping me.

Where am I? My heart started pounding. I clutched the blanket and tried to get my mind to work. And then it slammed into me: *My momma is dead. My momma is dead, and I am completely alone.*

I propped myself up on my elbows and looked around. I saw that I was in the top bunk in a row of empty bunk beds. *That's why the ceiling is so close, and I'm barricaded in,* I realized, *so I don't roll off.*

I looked beneath me and saw young elephants, some resting, others strolling casually around the room or munching on the leaves and hay piled in the corner.

More pieces came rushing back: the airplane, the heart monitor, the elephants bellowing. *I'm at the David Sheldrick Wildlife Trust.*

"You're awake!" Dafina appeared under the bed, grinning widely.

"Yes." Even that one word was a strain; my voice was weak, hoarse. I took a deep breath. "What happened?"

"You were very dehydrated and exhausted. You fainted, and we had to hydrate you through an IV."

I couldn't even remember the last time I had eaten. No wonder I had fainted.

"Thank you for helping me." I was about to say that I would be on my way when I realized I had nowhere to go.

The thought made me sit up abruptly. In my haste, I knocked my head against a beam in the ceiling. I bit my lip to keep from crying. *Don't cry, don't cry, don't cry— you're strong,* I repeated to myself, but the realization that I had nowhere to go made it hard to keep the tears back.

One or two escaped against my will, but fortunately Dafina, who was to the side of my bandaged cheek, did not see the tears trickle into the gauze.

"Ouch," Dafina said. "That looks like it hurt."

"Not really," I lied.

"Come down, Jama, there's someone here I know would love to see you."

"Mbegu!" I suddenly felt a wave of energy surge through me, sending me scrambling down the ladder.

She looked so small tucked in the corner under an orange-and-red blanket, sleeping peacefully. "She looks so...so..." I couldn't find the word.

Healthy? Not quite. *Strong?* That wasn't it, either.

"Alive and peaceful...," I said, and then I turned to Dafina. "Can I hug her?"

"Of course."

I walked slowly to her and tested her comfort by putting my hand on her back. She must have sensed my presence because her eyes opened. Immediately, she nuzzled her trunk up against me and started chirping, almost like a bird, only louder.

"She knows you," Dafina said. "She knows you saved her."

"Really?" I asked, even though I knew Dafina was right.

As if to confirm, Mbegu placed her trunk over me as I lay close beside her.

FORTY-EIGHT

Mbegu?" Dafina asked. "Is that what you call her?"

"I met her when she was very small, like a seed," I explained. "I wanted to watch her grow up."

"She's very lucky to have you. If it wasn't for you…" Neither of us needed or wanted her to finish that sentence.

We sat in silence a few minutes watching Mbegu take deep breaths. Truthfully, I was postponing whatever came next. Surely I would be asked to leave. Would someone give me a ride into Nairobi? All I knew of the city was that there were many people and shops.

I thought of how badly Nadira wanted to go there and dance in places like she'd seen on TV. Nadira! Another memory. Another heartbreak. Would I ever see her again?

Once more, I worked to shut down this line of thinking: my old life. I had to focus only on my future, such as it was. Maybe I could get a job making shoes in one of the markets, and maybe I could find a room to live in? My heart was speeding up again at the thought of what came now and next and after that. It was all a black hole.

"Jama, are you okay?"

"Yes, yes, I'm fine. I'm just...I'm just thinking about what will become of me."

"Well, about that..."

I was hardly listening because all I could think about was that I have nothing—no clothes, no money, no shoes other than Leku's sandals. I had nothing left of my mother or my home but memories. Bittersweet memories.

"What do you think, Jama?"

Lost in my thoughts, I'd missed everything Dafina had just said. "I'm sorry, can you repeat that?"

She smiled at me patiently. "We want you to live and work here, Jama."

It took a minute for that to register.

"Really?"

"Yes, really. We've been talking, the other caretakers and I, about everything that happened yesterday and how you dealt with it all. We're really impressed with you. Your compassion and dedication to saving Mbegu's life...well, we've never seen anything like it. Especially from someone so young."

"Thank—you—" I stammered. My face turned warm and it was as if the whole world was watching me, even though only Dafina was around.

"You have to be eighteen to join the team as a caretaker, but we'd like to invite you to be a junior caretaker."

"A junior caretaker...you mean looking after the elephants?" I asked.

Dafina nodded, a big smile on her face.

"Seriously?"

"Very serious," Dafina said. "You can work here after school. I know you're still in shock; it's okay if you need some time. I can only imagine the trauma of what happened."

"Are you saying that...I can *live* here?" I asked.

This made her laugh. "Yes! Where else would you live? We all live here so we can stay close to the animals. You can sleep right up there. Close to Mbegu." She pointed to the top bunk I had woken up in. "If you'd like."

"Really? Are you sure?" I put both hands over my heart. I was so happy and relieved by the overwhelming kindness that I thought I would burst. "Thank you, thank you, thank you so much," I said. "You're saving my life. With Baba and Momma gone, I had nowhere to go. I was going to be homeless."

"We wouldn't let that happen to you."

"Thank you," I said again, feeling I couldn't say it enough.

Dafina looked at me with sad eyes. I was very grateful that the staff at the Trust wanted me to stay with them when my own people didn't want me. I smiled, but though on some level I was happy, the throbbing ache deep in my chest remained.

"This is your home now, Jama," Dafina said. I stood up, and she let me wrap my arms around her waist. I squeezed tight, my cheek against her T-shirt, and I sobbed out of relief. I sobbed for Momma, and for Mbegu, and the guardian angels that had saved me.

"But for what it's worth," Dafina added when I stopped to take a breath, "no matter where you ended up, you would have survived. You're a survivor, just like Mbegu."

FORTY-NINE

Mbegu was getting stronger...and so was I. In the months since we arrived at the DSWT, we were both finding our way in our new lives. Mbegu's wounds were almost all healed, as was the cut on my cheek, but we both had deeper scars, too.

Sometimes I would exchange a look with Mbegu, and it was like we were having the same thought: *We've been through a lot.* Which is why it made me feel good to witness her thriving.

The mud baths made her happiest of all. I watched, delighted, as she kept trying to run through the thick sludge and tipped over. First she approached the task with determination, and now it was a big game, egged on by Dafina's laughter and mine. It was clear she loved the audience.

But it wasn't just the caretakers Mbegu enjoyed performing for, it was the other elephants, too. There were thirty orphaned elephants living at the Trust, all rescued from throughout Kenya, most of their mothers lost to poaching. Sometimes it broke my heart to see so many young elephants, all under five years old, who had lost their families. I knew what that felt like. But it also meant that Mbegu had twenty-nine new friends. She quickly became the star of the show.

Some other elephants, including her two best friends, Lullaby and Gacoki, ambled over to this end of the large pit, and Mbegu started another show just for them. She wriggled, rolled over, then sat on her hind legs and jiggled in the mud as she waved her small trunk around.

I could swear they were thoroughly amused by Mbegu's antics from the way they surrounded her and watched. Much to my dismay, however, the finale involved spraying a trunk full of water right at me. My uniform, a long green coat with THE DAVID SHELDRICK

WILDLIFE TRUST on the chest, was now splattered with mud, as usual.

Mbegu had come out of her shell more easily over our time here, but as for me, it was harder to open up to people and make friends. I had always been such a loner. There was also the sadness that clung to me like the smell of smoke.

But using Mbegu as my role model, I had managed to make two new friends myself.

First, Nathan, who at nineteen was the second youngest person at the Trust besides me. He was also the only white person at the Trust, at least that I'd seen up close, and sometimes I caught myself staring at his arms, which were so pale you could see rivers of blue vessels running through him.

My other friend, Hasana, was twenty-three. Hasana had left Nairobi to study in London and returned to work at DSWT. Sometimes I looked at her in awe; she was living my dream. She had stacks of textbooks from her studies in wildlife management that she let me read.

Nathan taught me to play checkers. Whenever we had a break from our duties—mucking the stalls and cleaning the bottles we used to feed the babies and other endless chores to keep the place running—we had marathon games. At first, he would let me win, but lately I won on my own skill.

When I spent time with Hasana and Nathan, and Mbegu, of course, I was happy. But these moments were chased by a feeling of guilt and a bit of shame. *How can I feel any joy when Momma is gone forever? When Baba is gone? When I will never see my people again? Is it heartless of me to sometimes feel happy?*

I didn't have time for these considerations at the moment, though. Playtime was over and I had to herd the elephants out of the mud. It was no easy feat getting a dozen rambunctious elephants back to their stalls.

FIFTY

You're really getting the hang of this," Dafina said to me. "All of it. I knew you'd be a natural."

I flushed with pride.

"Keep up the good work," she said as she patted my back and headed to the office.

I remember how tentative I was at first, too afraid to ask a question, but also so scared I would make a mistake and they would ask me to leave. There were a lot of books in the office about elephants and other animals, and I read them over and over, trying to learn what I could.

Nathan had found me one day the week before,

sitting under the desk, devouring a tattered paperback someone had left behind: a memoir by a woman named Jane Goodall about living with chimpanzees in Tanzania.

"You know you're a natural, right?" he'd said. "You can read all you want, but you're good with the animals. Patient. It's an instinct."

I'd beamed then just as I had when Dafina had paid me the same compliment. I was a flower soaking up their praise—and acceptance—like water.

"You've come such a long way," Nathan had said to me.

"I *have*?" I'd asked. He had no idea how one moment I felt I was getting better and the next my grief was suffocating me so tight I couldn't get a breath. But, as usual, I just smiled.

"When you first got here you were...you second-guessed yourself constantly; you were so insecure," he'd said.

I'd placed my free hand on my hip, cocked my head to one side, and paused, so he could tell he had said the wrong thing.

"I didn't mean that it was bad," he'd tried to back-pedal. "You were new and shy, that's all I meant to say. And now you're...confident."

"Hmmmmm." I'd rolled my eyes but let him have a half smile so he knew I was playing. I had learned this from Mbegu, from the way she would turn her face to the side when she wrestled with her friends so that they knew it was just a game, or how she would trot with her trunk between her legs when she was chasing after the birds, so they'd know she didn't want to hurt them.

He'd laughed at me, but then his tone turned earnest. "Seriously, look how well Mbegu is doing. I've never seen an animal get on the path to recovery so quickly, and that's largely because of you."

That part had caught me off guard, although something about it rang true.

Nathan came over now pushing a wheelbarrow filled with three-liter bottles of milk so we could get all the elephants fed. It was one of my favorite activities, watching their long pink tongues slurp up the milk we made for them every morning. It was also one of the messiest. By the end of the day, my uniform was always caked with mud and old milk and dung, of course. So much dung.

FIFTY-ONE

As usual, the day was so busy, I hardly noticed when the sun went down. But as soon as it did, as soon as I slowed down, came the dread.

This happened almost every night still. Because in the quiet of darkness, when I climbed into my bunk, I had a harder time keeping the dark thoughts at bay. Most nights I lay there, eyes closed but wide awake, thinking about Momma and Baba and home.

I wondered about Kokoo Naserian; who was collecting water for her? I thought of Momma's beans and worried that the leaves had probably turned brown and brittle and died just like her. I wondered if Nadira had been promised to Jehlani for marriage yet. I wondered what had become of the rest of the herd—Modoc and Lulu and the others.

And many nights I thought of Solo Mungu, too, wondering if he was still out there hurting the elephants.

I had told Dafina all about my suspicions. She was not surprised. She explained that this was a common practice, that many corrupt rangers got paid by the poachers to look away. I couldn't think of anything more evil than taking money to let animals die when your job is to protect them.

It got worse when she explained that even though she would report our suspicions to the authorities, it would be hard to stop him without hard proof. Which is what I was afraid of. At least she believed me, even if I had none. But still, we had no way of knowing how many more elephants had died on his watch. It haunted me.

When I finally fell asleep that night after tossing and turning under my plaid blanket, it was not for long. I was wrenched awake from a nightmare in which I was being chased by a man with dark sunglasses and I couldn't run fast enough.

Then Momma was screaming, "Get out of the way, Jama!"

Then more screams, so loud it was as if they came from inside my ears. Then a thud. A cry.

I woke up struggling to breathe, panting as if I really had been running at full speed through the bush.

Still shaken, I climbed down from my bunk and curled up by Mbegu's side. I rested my head on her stomach and felt the rise and fall of her breathing. It was soothing. Soothing the way I imagined floating on an ocean would be. Soothing like the way I remember Momma rocking me as a little girl.

"You are okay, Jama. You are okay." I spoke quietly to myself. My voice calmed me, but then my panic broke up into tiny pieces and flowed from me in tears.

Mbegu opened one eye, and then she lifted her trunk and tucked it around me.

I wondered, *Does she remember what happened to her mother? Does the memory play over and over in her head like it does in mine? Do elephants have nightmares?*

Snuggled next to Mbegu, I made a decision. I could still do something. I had to. Maybe it would stop the nightmares once and for all.

And besides, feeling sorry for myself was not going to save a single elephant. But I knew what could.

FIFTY-TWO

C an you help me send another letter?" I asked
Dafina the following morning.

"Of course." She looked a bit surprised. I
had only sent one letter since I arrived.

"I want to write to Kokoo Naserian again," I explained.

Later that day, when I had a short break from my
duties, I sat under a tree with the pen and paper Dafina
gave me and wrote to Kokoo Naserian.

> Dear Auntie,
>
> I'm sorry it's been so long since I've
> written. I miss you every day and wonder

how you are. I'm sure you must have been worried about me, and I should have written again sooner.

But you don't need to be concerned. I am safe. I am still loving it here at the Trust.

It's an honor to take care of orphaned and sick animals from all over Kenya. Right now, there are thirty baby elephants here and some other animals, too.

You would love these animals, Kokoo Naserian. They are playful and adorable. Dafina, she's my friend who works here, calls me "a natural."

The letter got longer and longer, as long as one of Kokoo Naserian's tales, as I went on to add many details about Mbegu and life at the Trust.

Finally, I got to the point of what I needed to ask her. I said it as plainly as I could and hoped that she would believe me. I told her how I believed that Solo Mungu was taking bribes from poachers to look the other way.

The last thing I wanted to do was put Kokoo Naserian in danger, but I knew she loved the elephants as much as I did.

I told her that the people at the Trust were going to investigate but that we still needed proof of his evildoing. Since she never missed a thing that happened in our village, I asked if she could keep her ears open to what was going on. If she learned about any more suspicious developments, it might lead us to the proof we needed. She was one person who was not afraid of him.

When I finished the letter, I read the whole thing out loud and it made me feel as though I were speaking with Kokoo Naserian. I imagined myself sitting with her under the stars glimmering in the sky, and listening to her endless stories. It was a memory that healed and hurt at the same time.

When I first wrote Kokoo Naserian a letter, my problem had been trying to figure out how to send it. I knew that she received letters from a cousin in Nairobi through Mrs. Wandera, our school headmistress, who often gave me the letters to deliver, so I'd mailed it to the school, which I'd have to do again now.

I knew that whoever took the letter to Kokoo Naserian would have to read it to her because she couldn't read. There was a time Baba used to read Kokoo Naserian her letters, then after he died, Momma or I read them for her. Now I was gone, too. I wondered who would read to her.

I didn't want this letter to somehow land in Solo Mungu's hands. But I was desperate.

I carefully wrote out Kokoo Naserian's name, CARE OF MRS. WANDERA, and the school address in big square letters in blue ink. I was pleased with the results. I had successfully imitated the handwriting and style of the letters I had delivered to Kokoo Naserian from her cousin. I figured that if it looked as if it was from her cousin, it wouldn't raise any suspicions.

I walked to the office and popped it in the Trust's post bag and prayed that Mrs. Wandera would give it to Nadira to deliver. Everyone knew she went to help her mother at the market after school and she passed near our manyatta on the way. Or rather, the manyatta where Kokoo Naserian now lived alone.

I didn't mind Nadira reading my letter to Kokoo Naserian because if there was someone who could keep a secret, it was Nadira.

I wondered if she would be upset that I didn't write her, too, or if she missed me at all. We had been growing apart, it was true, but she was still my first friend, and that would always matter.

FIFTY-THREE

Every day after I sent the letter, I wondered if Kokoo Naserian had received it. Since she couldn't read or write, I wasn't expecting to hear back, but I hoped just hearing from me made her happy.

Then, two weeks later, I looked up to find Nathan waving and calling to me. I was out at the mud baths for an afternoon play session with the elephants.

"You have a visitor!"

My insides felt like they were replaced with feathers. Who could it be?

Only Kokoo Naserian knew where I was. Surely the old woman hadn't traveled all the way to Nairobi. Perhaps she had sent someone to see me on her behalf? Perhaps her cousin who lived in Nairobi? Had my people missed me and come to apologize? Did they want me back? The thoughts raced.

I made a quick stop to change out of my gum boots and wash my hands and then headed to reception. The staff member on duty pointed at a side room.

The door was slightly ajar, and just before I stepped through it, I heard a familiar voice. A cold chill crept up the back of my neck, but it was too late to turn around. I found myself standing before none other than Solo Mungu.

"Come in, Jama," he said with a snarl disguised as a smile. "Everyone back home sends their greetings."

I stepped forward slightly and swallowed my fear in a big gulp. I hoped Solo Mungu and his two companions didn't notice.

Jama, be brave. Jama, ACT brave, I thought.

Solo Mungu in his camouflage regalia and dark glasses took up all the space in the small room. Everyone was close enough to touch.

"Good afternoon, Mr. Mungu, and how is everyone back home?" My voice sounded squeaky. All I could think was that he had somehow learned what I wrote to Kokoo Naserian—my accusation. Someone in the crowd must have told him what I had said that day, when I said it was his fault the poachers came and Momma died. Had he come to threaten me?

FIFTY-FOUR

T ake a seat," Solo Mungu said, as though it was his place to offer hospitality.

I remained standing. I was closest to the door and that wasn't going to change.

He was watching me intently, lips curled. He stood up, walked over to the bulletin board hanging on the wall, and peered at the photographs and notices.

With his back to me he spoke. "Hmmmm...I see you and your friend are getting along well."

He tapped a photograph of me sitting beside Mbegu with her trunk around my shoulders. It had been taken a few days after we arrived at the Trust. Mbegu was still covered in bruises, and her eyes were flat; you could see the grief in mine, too. In the photo we're clinging to each other for dear life, which captures exactly how it was those first weeks.

I looked down at my feet. Leku's sandals. I'd changed into them when I left the mud bath. I wore them every day so that they were, by this point, worn and ripped, but they were all I had of home. I kept my focus on my feet, feeling Solo's eyes on me, even through his glasses.

"We are here because we are looking for your friend." Solo Mungu's words startled me.

Friend? Who? What is he talking about?

"Your friend Lekuton. Apparently, he's run away, and his mother and sisters are going crazy with worry."

Well, you don't look very worried. "I don't know where he is. The last time I saw him was the day after Momma died."

"Aaah, so you agree he is your friend?" He turned around and looked at me from over the top of his glasses.

So it was a trick question.

"Well, actually, no. He isn't my friend," I said, then for some strange reason felt like a traitor. "We just went to the same school."

I wondered what Leku had said to his mother to make her think we were friends.

Solo Mungu's gaze bored into me. I stared back, determined now not to let him scare me. I had done nothing wrong. I didn't know where Leku was, even though I was worried for him. As for my calling him a poacher, if that's really what this was about, I was right.

"Well, gentlemen, I think we are finished here," Solo Mungu said, and the two other men stood up. "Apparently Leku is not here, and this young lady does not know where he is. I will report back to his mother."

Anger boiled up in me. Solo Mungu had not come because he cared for Leku, but because his wife had asked him to.

I stepped out of the room and stood aside so that the three men could exit. As Solo Mungu walked past me, he stopped and raised his sunglasses so he could lock his coal-black eyes on mine. He spoke so the others couldn't hear. "Look after yourself, little girl. There are evil men out there ... like poachers."

I stood still as he spoke, breath trapped in my lungs.

Then he suddenly burst out laughing, causing me to jump. He seemed tickled by my reaction. "I should know, I'm a ranger—right?" He guffawed, showing his big white teeth.

He walked away laughing while I stood in the doorway, completely frozen but for my racing heart.

FIFTY-FIVE

In the days after Solo Mungu's visit I started jumping at my own shadow. Hasana and Nathan knew all about my suspicions and agreed that Solo oozed evil, but they reassured me that he would not get to me at the Trust. I was safe here.

And they were probably right, but on the odd day that we ventured beyond the grounds, it gave me anxiety.

Which explained why I was nervous and jumpy when I went to the market with Hasana the next Saturday. She said it wasn't really a market because it was very small, but in comparison to the paltry stalls back home, it was enormous and filled with so much to see.

It was our day off, and we were wandering somewhat aimlessly. I wished I knew the name of the man who sold Momma's sandals so I could go visit him.

Hasana said it would be impossible to find him without a name or even knowing exactly where his stall was located. "Do you know how many people are selling shoes in this city?" she said.

I couldn't have guessed. I wondered if he knew Momma was gone; he must by now. I wondered if he had found someone else to make sandals. They wouldn't be as beautiful, that's for sure. I liked the idea that there were still people, all over the world, wearing Momma's shoes.

"This is pretty, no?" Hasana said, running her hands over a beautiful piece of fabric. She had started sewing skirts in her spare time. She held it up for further inspection, but I was distracted, noticing the man standing just past her.

He had stopped at every stall we had. Tall and broad, he could pass for Solo Mungu's brother. He wasn't buying anything, but neither were we. All the same, I wondered why a man was hovering around stalls selling fabric, beads, and earrings for women. At one point I caught his eye, and he smiled at me. It was a friendly smile, but I wasn't convinced.

"I think that man is following us," I whispered to Hasana.

"Who?" she asked, spinning around to see who was there.

"Don't look now. But the tall man in the white shirt."

"But why would anyone—" Hasana stopped abruptly. "Solo Mungu?" she asked.

"Well, not him, but maybe one of his men." It sounded far-fetched when I said it out loud.

"I'm telling you, he has no reason to hurt you, so please don't worry. I hope one day we can get the proof we need against him. But until then, maybe he truly did just want to know what happened to his son?" She reached out to rub my arm to reassure me. "Now look, this one or this one?" She held two beaded earrings up to her delicate ears.

I put Solo Mungu and the man in the white shirt out of my mind and helped her decide between the two. After she made her purchase, she wanted to go shop for more fabric. I loved going to the market with my friend, but it required a good deal of patience since she could shop for fabrics for hours upon hours.

Meanwhile, I was hungry and craving my favorite treat whenever I came to the market—thin bread covered in tomato sauce and cheese and baked in a small woodstove. It was Hasana who'd introduced me to this food—pizza—that she'd first had in London.

As if she could read my mind, she turned to me. "I suppose you want to go to Sal's."

That was the name of the man, an immigrant from Italy, who made my new favorite food.

I nodded, smiling, pleased to be known so well. "I will meet you back at the Trust?"

She nodded, already distracted by a sparkling stream of glass beads.

I turned to make my way along a narrow passage between stalls, when a large tourist group swarmed by vendors came walking toward me. Seeing so many pale faces was still a novelty, and I stopped to stare. The vendors formed a tight circle around the tourists and held out their wares. They jostled one another as they shouted out prices and spoke at the same time:

"Good price. This one, fifty shillings. Okay, forty-five."

"Madam, this one buy, just forty. Special price for you."

"Take for thirty shillings."

For a moment I had to stop when bodies jammed around me. I changed direction, deciding to try and squeeze around the mob rather than through it.

I passed a small veranda where a woman was braiding the hair of a little girl who wailed loudly. Somehow I got disoriented in the maze of stalls. Even after all this time I could still become overwhelmed by the size of the market, dozens of tightly packed stalls and stands overflowing with goods and animals and people, laid out like a small, disorganized city. And everyone speaking so many different languages.

Before I left home, I'd only ever heard Maa and Swahili, but here in the market there was also English and French and Mandarin from all corners, like so many birdcalls. I looked around, trying to get my bearings, and realized I'd ended up in a narrow alleyway dotted with garbage and boxes.

I was trying to decide which direction to turn when I sensed a figure coming out of the shadows toward me, faster and faster.

FIFTY-SIX

Shock prevented me from screaming.

Before I even had time to flinch or duck, the figure had pulled me into a tight embrace, pressing me against the soft cushion of her chest.

"It *is* you, it *is* you, my Jama. I can't believe it!"

The fear and panic gave way first to surprise and then relief and then to utter joy. I almost fainted for the second time in my life to find myself in the arms of Busara Kandenge.

"What are you doing here, Momma Busara?"

"I am here visiting my nephew. He is getting married, and I wanted to get a few things for the wedding, and I thought I saw you. But I wasn't sure if I was imagining it! What are the chances? And here you are. It is a miracle, praise Enkai."

She held on to both my shoulders and looked me up and down. "You've grown so much. Such a beautiful young woman."

Tears sprung from her eyes.

"It is Enkai's will that I ran into you so that I could beg for forgiveness. Mtoto wangu. I'm so sorry, my child. Please forgive me. Since you left, Aluna keeps me awake at night. She asks me why I have abandoned you. I should have done more to help you. I am so sorry."

Everything had happened so fast I didn't know what to say. I was still trying to catch my breath and come down from danger-alert mode. The shock of coming face-to-face with Busara Kandenge, not Solo Mungu, left me completely confused and disoriented.

"Jama, will you have tea with me, so we can talk?"

I agreed and we walked a few yards to a little tea shop with a few wooden tables. Busara Kandenge couldn't take her eyes off me, and I felt shy in her gaze. "Please tell me how you are. Tell me everything."

So I did. I told her about my months at the Trust, my

work, and my new friends. I told her that Mbegu was thriving.

"What about you? You are happy?"

"I am." I realized it was true.

"I am happy for you. But...but I think it's time for you to come home."

Her words caught me by surprise. It was one thing to ask for my forgiveness, quite another to expect me to go back.

What would I be going back to? I had a new life at the Trust. I was happy with Mbegu and the other animals. I couldn't imagine myself back at our manyatta, especially without Momma.

I took a sip of my tea to bide time. But I already knew my answer.

"I can never come back, Momma Busara. I have a new home now. I forgive you. I forgive everyone, but please understand."

She looked at me as if she didn't know quite what to make of me. A look I was generally used to. "Well, could I visit you when I'm here in town? Take you to tea?"

"I'd like that, Momma Busara. Very much."

"And you know you are welcome to come home, anytime."

But the truth was, I *was* home. The Trust was my home now.

She reached over to hug me again in her thick arms. "Oh, Jama, you are so much like your mother, strong and courageous. I know Aluna is watching over you. And that she is bursting with pride."

FIFTY-SEVEN

That night, after running into Busara Kandenge, was the first one I didn't have a nightmare since my mother died.

I saw Momma in a dream, but it was good; she was wearing a long white robe and laughing and singing. All the next day the same melody was stuck in my head, and I found myself humming "Malaika," and it made me feel close to her.

I was busy refilling the hay supply in each of the stalls when I heard a commotion near the entrance. A DSWT truck zoomed up the driveway, spinning red dust into the air. The staff dropped everything and rushed over the same as they'd done the day Mbegu arrived. In the truck's bed was an impossibly small elephant covered in blood.

By now I was used to the drill of injured animals arriving, but it was no less heartbreaking. I was sad that an elephant had lost its mother or, as often happened, had been injured itself. But at the same time, I felt pleased because it meant one more elephant had been rescued. I joined the team circling the new arrival.

Everyone knew that I had a calming effect on the elephants, so I was always called when a new calf was brought in. While the medical team got to work, I stepped into my role, looking the calf in the eye and speaking in soothing tones.

"You'll be fine. You are in safe hands," I murmured gently.

When I took in the calf's injuries up close, I was filled with rage. There was a jagged, gaping gash where a wire had dug into its flesh.

"Another snare!" Matthew said, not even bothering to keep the anger out of his voice.

Poachers used these to trap animals, a wire attached to a piece of wood that would wrap around their leg. It was cruel and painful and resulted in deep cuts.

Sometimes children would accidentally get trapped in these snares, too.

From the way the wound was torn, I could tell the elephant had struggled to free himself, and the more he struggled the tighter the wire gripped him, which was exactly how the snare was supposed to work.

As the other caretakers took the vitals of the calf and monitored his heartbeat, Matthew grabbed large, blue-handled pliers and snipped the wire off the calf's leg.

"Looks like we got to him just in time," Dafina said. "He's lucky he was even found."

And indeed, the calf was lucky. Because often animals that got caught in snares died from starvation before they could be rescued.

After the calf's heartbeat had stabilized and the wound had been cleaned, Matthew asked me to rub green clay on the elephant's leg to help it heal.

As I massaged the clay into his leg, I told our new arrival a story about a cheeky and playful elephant called Mbegu who he would soon get to meet. As I spoke to him his eyes opened a bit more. It might have been my imagination, but I saw the sadness in them lift away slowly.

I was thinking of what might be a good name for our new friend when Dafina burst into the room. The man who had brought in the calf followed close behind. He was stocky, with ginger hair and a small scar on his face.

"Jama, listen to this." Dafina turned back to the man excitedly. "Tell her what you just told me, Raj."

"About the poachers getting caught?" he asked.

Dafina didn't wait for him to reply. She broke the news to me herself. "Solo Mungu has been arrested!"

FIFTY-EIGHT

I looked from Dafina to the man, trying to process this shocking information.

"Do you know him?" Raj raised his thick orange brows at me.

"He worked in the reserve close to Jama's home," Dafina said. "She's the one who first told us what happened—she saw him being paid off months ago—and we reported it. That's what started the investigation. Jama is basically a hero!"

She beamed at me, but I was still two steps behind, trying to put the pieces together. It's like that when the thing you've wanted most happens; it takes time for your brain to believe it's real.

"What happened?" I finally found my voice.

"Well, we found the elephant I brought in just now in the Naibunga Conservancy," Raj explained.

It was an echo of the past, of home, to hear the name of this place again.

"We heard that some poachers were caught there a couple of nights ago. Apparently some rangers had information about possible poachers in the area—I guess that's thanks to you, I see—and they were coming so they lay in wait. When the poachers arrived, the rangers opened fire, and the poachers shot back. In the exchange two poachers were caught but two got away."

"And the elephants?" I asked.

"Fortunately, they got away in the commotion. But today this poor chap was found in a snare not far from where the shootout took place." He looked at the calf, who had started to swish his tail. "We suspect he lost his mum as the herd escaped, and he must have gotten caught in the snare as he wandered alone."

Anger bubbled inside me. "And Solo Mungu? Was he one of the men caught?"

"No. The captured poachers are the ones who

implicated Solo Mungu. They said he told them when the rangers were on patrol, so the poachers knew when the coast was clear."

I smiled in satisfaction. "I knew I was right about him."

Dafina returned my smile like we were in a competition to see who could grin the biggest. "Of course you were! We just had to be patient. We knew we could catch him sooner or later. Justice feels good, doesn't it?"

It did.

Raj chimed in. "That Mungu guy had such a formidable reputation as an effective ranger, only hard evidence will put him away. Even after the poachers implicated him, no one believed them. It was the poachers' word against Mungu, so you can guess who everyone believed."

"Then how did he get arrested?" Dafina asked.

"Would you believe his own son and a very old woman came forward and backed the poachers' story?"

My heart jumped.

"I mean I can see the old woman selling him out, but his own son?" the man added, shaking his head in disbelief.

"Kokoo Naserian and Leku," I spoke quietly, almost to myself.

So Kokoo Naserian must have gotten my letter. I felt a sense of triumph. It wasn't exactly hard proof, maybe, but it helped. And Leku? I was proud of him for going up against his father. That took incredible strength.

"Do you know the son? Is he your friend?" Dafina asked me.

Without hesitating, I heard myself say, "Yes, Leku is my friend."

FIFTY-NINE

Time moves differently when you work outside every day. My clock used to be set to the school calendar. Now, I was more attuned to nature's timing: the sun's place in the sky, the fullness of the moon, the rainy and dry seasons.

I'd come to the Trust before the rainy season started, and the months now melted away into the sludgy gray of torrential rains. The elephants loved it—all the better for mud baths. But me, not as much. I was tired of soggy toes and fingers.

And yet, I remained giddy about the justice brought

to Solo Mungu. He'd already begun serving a twenty-five-year prison term. The government was determined to make an example of him to discourage poachers.

So, but for the waterlogged days, life was good. Little did I know it was about to get even better.

I was in the office counting the payments from the day's visitors. This is how the Trust made money, charging tourists a small fee for the chance to look at and feed the elephants.

It was always fun to see the looks on their faces when the staff paraded the elephants in front of the long line of people waiting for them—although often I couldn't even see their faces, hidden as they were behind their cameras and phones that they barely put down. I wanted to say to them, *Just enjoy this.* But I never did.

Nathan interrupted my count by dropping a brown box on the desk.

"What's this?" I asked.

"A package. It came in the post for you today."

I'd never gotten a package. Even without knowing what was inside, it was a thrill. I ran my finger over the words in black ink: JAMA ANYANGO, C/O THE DAVID SHELDRICK WILDLIFE TRUST.

I reached into a drawer and found a pair of scissors. I stared at the package for a minute more before I cut into it. But then I couldn't wait any longer; the anticipation and curiosity were killing me.

The first thing I noticed was the fabric. I instantly recognized the familiar red-and-yellow pattern. It was my shuka! The new one I wore for the Eunoto.

I brought it to my face. The scent of Momma and the inside of our enkajijik filled my nostrils. It was the smell of smoke and the coconut oil Momma used on her skin. I traced the pattern on the beautiful fabric, fighting tears but losing.

There was something else in the box. I recognized that, too, immediately. It was the small leather pouch that Baba used to carry with him everywhere he went. After he died Momma had kept it close to her.

Stuck to it was a note from Busara Kandenge.

I wanted you to have these things. So you can always think of home.

As if that wasn't enough, there was more.

SIXTY

I noticed a white envelope at the bottom. My name was written on the front in block letters. Inside was a letter neatly folded into thirds, filled with the same block lettering in thick blue ink.

DEAR ELEPHANT GIRL (JOKE),

I SUPPOSE YOU HAVE HEARD BY NOW THAT MY FATHER IS IN JAIL. YOU WERE RIGHT ABOUT HIM, AND I'M SORRY FOR EVERYTHING HE DID. I HEAR THAT YOUR FRIEND MBEGU IS DOING WELL AND YOU ARE, TOO—YOU ARE LIVING AT THE DAVID SHELDRICK WILDLIFE TRUST. BUSARA KANDENGE

TOLD ME THAT SHE FOUND YOU AND THAT YOU ARE HAPPY. SHE GOES TO VISIT KOKOO NASERIAN EVERY DAY AND SO DO I SOMETIMES AFTER SCHOOL. THE BOYS MAKE FUN OF ME—"WHY DO YOU HANG OUT WITH THAT OLD LADY?"—BUT SHE HAS GOOD STORIES AND SHE IS KIND TO ME. SHE PAYS ME SOME MONEY TO MILK THE GOAT AND TO COLLECT EGGS FOR HER. I AM SAVING UP FOR A MOTORBIKE WHEN I MOVE.

I AM GOING TO LIVE WITH MY UNCLE, A JEWELRY MAKER IN MAGADI. MY MOTHER SAYS THAT WITH MY DAD NOT AROUND I NEED TO BE WITH A MAN. SHE ALSO CAN'T AFFORD ANOTHER MOUTH SINCE WE DON'T HAVE MY FATHER'S SALARY ANYMORE.

I AM SOMETIMES SCARED TO GO OFF AND START A NEW LIFE SOMEWHERE I'VE NEVER BEEN. I TRIED IT BEFORE. WHEN THINGS GOT BAD WITH MY FATHER, I RAN AWAY INTO THE BUSH. I THOUGHT I COULD SURVIVE THERE ON MY OWN AND THAT EVEN THE HYENAS WOULD BE BETTER THAN MY FATHER. BUT I ONLY LASTED FIVE NIGHTS. THEN I THINK ABOUT HOW YOU MADE A NEW LIFE, AND I HAVE THE STRENGTH TO TRY AGAIN. BUT IN A

REAL HOUSE THIS TIME. HA! WHEN I TOLD KOKOO
NASERIAN THAT I WAS LEAVING THE VILLAGE, SHE
SAID, "IT IS THE EYE THAT HAS TRAVELED THAT IS
CLEVER." I THINK THAT IS HER GIVING ME HER
BLESSING.

MY UNCLE COMES TO NAIROBI A LOT ON
BUSINESS AND I WILL BE JOINING HIM. SO I WAS
THINKING…MAYBE I COULD SEE YOU ON ONE
OF THOSE TRIPS? I HOPE SO. YOU WILL SEE THAT I
HAVE GROWN VERY TALL, SO YOU CAN'T CALL ME
SHORT HIPPO ANYMORE. AND I BELIEVE YOU HAVE
IN YOUR POSSESSION A PAIR OF SANDALS THAT
BELONG TO ME. I'M CERTAIN THAT YOU HAVE NOT
THROWN THEM AWAY SO I WILL BE COMING TO GET
THEM (JOKE).

I REALLY HOPE TO HEAR BACK FROM YOU AND
TO SEE YOU ONE DAY SOON.

YOUR FRIEND, LEKU

"What are you smiling like that about?"

I had forgotten that Nathan was still there, standing in the doorframe.

He watched me tightly clutching the shuka, the pouch, and the letter.

"Nothing, nothing," I said shyly. "Just memories from my old life."

But what I should have said was: *Everything*.

SIXTY-ONE

I t's your very first date!" Hasana cooed for the tenth time in so many minutes.

"It's not a date." I was becoming increasingly irritated but tried not to show it. A part of me wished I hadn't shared with her that I was going to meet Leku.

But I had told her all about the letters we'd been exchanging for a full year. I even read parts to her out loud late at night, as we sat in front of the fireplace. Not the romantic bits, never those, that was just for me.

"I went on my first date when I was around your age, too," Hasana said. "Orlando Omotola. We had to sneak away since both of our families would have forbidden it. That's part of what made it exciting, I think, because he was actually rather boring, and I realized that soon enough."

It made me wonder how Momma would feel about this. *Would she forbid it, or would she encourage me?*

This was the impossible struggle of being an orphan, always having to guess at what your parents would think about your life. I hoped they would be proud. And part of me is certain that they would approve of Leku, the sullen bully who grew up into the kind of boy who quoted poems in his letters.

Thinking of what he wrote in his last letter—a poem about the night longing for the sun—gives me a fluttery feeling that is love or nerves or both.

Leku's move to Magadi ended up getting delayed because his mother got sick—a bad bout of malaria—and he stayed to take care of his sisters. It was only when she was better that he went to his uncle's and only now that we'd, finally, be able to meet.

Today.

There was so much buildup, though. The butterflies in my stomach had multiplied so much over the months that I knew when I finally tried to talk to him, they might well burst out of my throat.

"Which ones?" I turned to Hasana and asked her which neck beads would go better with the white blouse I'd borrowed from her.

"The red ones. Easy."

I fastened them around my neck and took one more look. Would Leku still see the skinny twelve-year-old girl, or would he be shocked to see me now? Sometimes, I was still surprised by the young woman looking back at me in the mirror.

"Now, go, go, you're going to be late," Hasana said. "And here, you'll need this." She thrust a tattered umbrella in my hands.

It wasn't even the rainy season yet, but the rain poured out of the slate-colored sky with a continuous pattering that usually meant it was going to last the whole day. Rain meant the gravel road leading from the Trust was waterlogged so I would have to slosh through a sludge of mud to get to the bus stop on the main road.

On top of that, we'd agreed to meet outside, in the market by the benches at the corner of Queens Bazaar grocery store near Sal's. The location was no accident. I had this idea that I might introduce Leku to pizza.

But the plan was seeming more ill-advised by the

second. By the time I got halfway down the driveway, the secondhand suede pumps I'd bought with Hasana yesterday would turn brown and soggy.

Perhaps the rain was a warning, a sign that I should stay home. Perhaps everything going wrong was a sign of things to come. I could take off this white blouse and put my uniform back on and go out and snuggle with Mbegu under a blanket, as I had hundreds of other nights.

SIXTY-TWO

Maybe I shouldn't go." I didn't realize I had spoken out loud until Hasana's head popped up beside mine in the mirror.

Her eyes opened wide. "Of course you're going!" she said.

"I...I...can't. It's raining. I'm sure we can meet up another time."

"Since when did rain stop you?" She placed her hands on her hips as if daring me to reply. "Jama, who practically joins the elephants in their mud bath, is today put off by a drizzle of rain?"

"But after all the effort I put into straightening my

hair, it will shrink in the rain. What's the point?" Even I knew I sounded whiny, but I couldn't help feeling sorry for myself.

"Jama, you're going!"

"But my shoes will get muddy and—"

"No more buts," Hasana interrupted me. "All you have to do is carry your new shoes in your bag and change when you get on the bus." She picked the red shoes off the floor and held them up. "Or even better still, I'll walk up to the main road with you, then you can change into these at the bus stop and I'll bring back your muddy boots."

"What if he doesn't show up?" I asked, then when she raised her brows at me I hurriedly added, "I mean, he could get caught in the rain or something."

"Well, then you'll come back." She found a plastic bag and popped my shoes inside. "It's not like you're traveling miles and miles to meet the love of your life. He's just a friend, right? So if he doesn't show up, you come back home and life goes on. Simple."

I nodded because I had no choice. Hasana had set a trap for me, and I walked right into it. If I didn't agree with her, I would be admitting that meeting Leku was a bigger deal than I was willing to acknowledge.

My anxiety worsened as the bus approached the market. I was sweating despite the chill in the air, and I couldn't even blame the rain for the soggy patches on my shirt, as it had stopped for the moment.

As usual, the market was a buzzing hive of activity. I made my way to the meeting spot. My eyes scanned over and around bodies searching for a square head I assumed would stand above the rest. When I didn't see him, my heart started sinking, like an old balloon gradually losing air.

I stopped by a bench under the shade of an umbrella-shaped acacia tree. I decided against sitting down. My nervous energy was better spent pacing. On my fifth turn to the far bench and back is when I saw him.

He had his back to me, but I knew the shape of that head. I started walking toward him, and as I drew closer, the teenager before me, with wide square shoulders and a bald head, transformed back into a much shorter boy with a dirty school uniform and mischievous grin.

Suddenly I was eight again, scrawny and knock-kneed, struggling to carry water from the river.

I hadn't been sure how seeing Leku would make me feel....Sad? Scared? Regretful? But it turns out it wasn't any one feeling, it was a downpour of so many of them, washing over me, and like a cleansing rain, what was left was a warm sensation running through my whole body. It was a sensation that took me so much by surprise that I burst into laughter, which drew curious expressions from the people around me, but I didn't care.

I ran up to Leku just as he turned and saw me coming. Without thinking, I threw my arms out to hug him, then I caught myself and stopped, embarrassed by my eagerness. My arms dropped to my sides, and my face felt as though it was on fire.

Leku smiled at me, the gap in his teeth making him all the more handsome.

I had rehearsed my greeting a thousand times, but when the time came, the words stayed in my mouth.

I was too embarrassed for having almost hugged him to explain that I was excited because seeing him had reminded me of home. I couldn't find the words to tell him I was happy because I had just realized that memories of my past—of our village and Momma and Shaba and Baba—didn't make me sad anymore. I was happy because of how far I'd come, how much I'd over-come, and how the future didn't scare me at all. In fact, I was excited to see what it would bring.

Say something, Jama. To my relief, the words finally came out of my mouth as I had planned.

"Hello, tall hippo," I said.

He reached for my hand. "Hello there, elephant girl."

EPILOGUE

When my eighteenth birthday came around, I got a beautiful checkers set from Nathan, a homemade skirt from Hasana, and from Dafina, a promotion.

Now that I was old enough, I could officially become an elephant keeper. It was an excellent moment when I put on my very own green jacket, so crisp and clean, with my name right on the front in a delicate cursive. It gave me the same puffed-up feeling that getting all A's gave me.

Dafina looked at me with the same pride I felt inside as I strutted in my new jacket, all smiles.

"Congratulations, Jama. Maybe you'll have my job one day soon," she said with a wink.

I knew she was only kidding—at least for the moment—but something lodged inside me when she spoke those words, a vision that one day I could be the head keeper here at the Trust.

But for the moment, other than the title and the new jacket, not much had changed day to day. I kept the stalls and sleeping quarters clean for the animals. I fed them, bathed them, and evaluated their behavior. When new orphans were rescued, I comforted them.

And there was another bittersweet duty: releasing elephants back into the wild. The first time we took an elephant out to reintegrate, I had only been at the Trust a few months. I suppose the day Mwashoti left was the day that I first realized Mbegu might one day leave the Trust, too.

Dafina reminded me that this was a good thing; the end goal of our work was to return elephants where they belonged. I didn't understand how they could possibly survive after months and, sometimes, years with us, but Dafina explained that their survival instincts would kick in and they would learn how to take care of themselves from other elephants, just as they would have growing up in the bush.

And we didn't simply turn them away one day; it was a gradual process where the elephants would leave the Trust with caretakers for field trips through the bush, and each time venture farther and farther.

There the keepers encouraged them to interact with wild herds so that a member of the herd might form a friendship and welcome a new member. The babies would start to learn about behavior and how to survive and get used to having more independence. At night they still came back to the Trust, but over time—a period of a few weeks or months, depending on the animal—they would be ready to stay with their new adopted family.

As she told me this, all those years ago, I was watching Mbegu play with Lullaby, and even though I knew animals belonged in the wild, it was hard to imagine that it was better than this, the safety of the Trust and all the love here.

So when the day finally came for Mbegu to be let out in the wild, I woke up with a throbbing pain deep inside me, in my soul. Before I was fully awake, it rose in my chest, and it took me a few minutes to remember why I felt so sad. It was the same pain I felt when Momma died, and I realized I had not felt it for a while.

Time had healed me, but the scars were still tender.

At breakfast, Hasana and Nathan and the other caretakers joked around to lighten my mood and the occasion.

"How many times do you think Mbegu will be back?" asked Hasana. Often the elephants wandered back to the Trust after they were let back into the wild. It took a few days or weeks before they finally left for good.

"Mbegu will probably follow us right back home," Nathan joked, and everyone laughed.

I tried to laugh because I knew what they were trying to do, but tears still welled up in my eyes before I could stop them.

"I'm sorry," I apologized to Nathan, who looked embarrassed because his joke had backfired.

"Dear girl, it's okay." Hasana rubbed my back while Adan and the other caretakers backed away to give me space. "Like I said before, we can wait another week or two if you're not ready to say goodbye."

"No." I sniffled. "She's ready and we've waited long enough."

Mbegu had been venturing farther alone each time we'd taken her out the last few weeks. She was curious about the world, just as she had been when she was a baby, poking around and exploring wherever we took her. She seemed at home in the bush, happy, and there was a herd of about twelve elephants roaming the southern part of Nairobi National Park that had embraced her. How could they not? She was Mbegu, impossible not to love.

Reminding myself of this, I swallowed the lump in my throat and prepared as best as I could to say goodbye.

We drove for about two hours into Nairobi National Park with Mbegu in the back of a truck. Now that she was a whopping fifteen hundred pounds, we needed a much bigger truck than the one we'd arrived in all those years ago.

Eventually we spotted the herd, Mbegu's future family, chomping on the leaves of acacia trees. The adults broke branches and lowered them to their young. We stopped, jumped out of the truck, and untied Mbegu. I sensed she knew it was time to say goodbye because instead of starting to explore her new surroundings as she usually did, she didn't move.

When we tried to encourage her to go off and explore, she wrapped her trunk around my neck and refused to budge. I wanted to hold on for dear life, too. I wanted to call this whole thing off, but that would have been selfish.

I remembered how Momma worried about me being unable to cope in the world without her. And to think at the time I thought she worried too much. I hadn't understood that it was natural to feel that way about a loved one. But although Momma worried, she knew that we would not always be together. I remembered how she told me that life was such that loved ones parted. It's what I reminded myself when I learned that Kokoo Naserian died a few months ago. It was just a fact of life.

But the stabbing pain in my chest started up again nonetheless. It was the pain of my heart and my head at war with each other.

I gently pulled Mbegu's trunk from around my neck. She was about my height now, so I could look straight into her eyes.

"I'm going to miss you so much," I told her. "But you'll be happiest in the wild with your own people." I laughed at myself. "I mean your own species. You know what I mean. Oh, this is even harder than I thought."

I took a deep breath and tried to compose myself. The elephant I called Luna, as a nod to my mother, looked at us expectantly. Luna was the one that had taken a special interest in Mbegu. It was Luna I trusted to keep Mbegu safe.

"I'll never forget you, okay?" I continued, trying to be strong for Mbegu. Of course I knew elephants communicate in a different way—they didn't speak our language—but still, I felt Mbegu understood. We had always understood each other. "You're going to do great, Mbegu," I said.

I tried to be grateful for this chance to say goodbye. We don't always get that.

As if reading my mind, Mbegu raised her trunk to my face and planted a big smacker on my cheek. I burst out laughing. She did understand we were saying goodbye. "Oh, Mbegu, I love you with all my heart."

With that, I backed away and joined Hasana and the others who were watching from a short distance. Luna ambled over. She was much bigger than Mbegu and towered over her as she approached. My heart skipped a beat as Mbegu craned her neck to look up at Luna, waiting with bated breath for what would happen next. They stood before each other, waving their ears ever so slightly, in a staring contest or the world's most tranquil showdown. Then Luna raised her trunk and touched it to Mbegu's ear, then the other.

The image of this greeting was blurry to me, given I was watching through a film of tears.

After Luna sniffed Mbegu's ears, she placed her trunk close to Mbegu's and began to swing it back and forth, knocking it gently against Mbegu's. Mbegu followed her lead and soon their trunks were bumping up against each other like high-fives in slow motion. Luna curled her trunk around Mbegu's, and they stood entangled for what felt like hours. In reality, it was probably no more than a minute. When they finally untied themselves, Luna swung her massive trunk in a big, sweeping motion toward the herd. Mbegu began to walk toward them, Luna following close behind.

"There she goes," I said, my voice high pitched as I swallowed back the flurry of panic that I may never see Mbegu again and there was nothing I could do about it.

"Yes!" the team cheered, happy to see Mbegu stroll off to join a new family. I wished I felt their joy, but a black cloud settled over me.

Mbegu turned around to look at me one last time. I sensed she was smiling, so I smiled back and summoned the will to lift my heavy arm and wave goodbye.

During the drive back to the Trust, a slideshow of Mbegu and me played in my mind, all my favorite memories in a constant loop. I was happy that the team didn't try to cheer me up; we just rode in silence. I had already decided I would skip dinner and go straight to bed. It would be my first night without Mbegu beneath me, and I wanted to get it over with.

But as we pulled down the road to the Trust, a familiar figure was standing by the gate. Leku. He'd come all the way from Magadi. We'd written to each other over the years and saw each other when he came to town once a month, but he wasn't supposed to visit again until the end of the summer.

The truck stopped at the entrance, and Leku called out over the roar of the engine.

"I knew today would be a hard day. I'm here to cheer you up!"

I jumped out of the truck and hugged him. Unlike our first meeting, I didn't hesitate when I launched myself into his arms these days.

Turns out, Leku was there to do more than just cheer me up, or at least he had a dramatic plan for doing so. He asked me to marry him.

I stood there staring at him, with his lopsided eager smile, and I remembered Momma's words from all those years ago so vividly it was like she was there, whispering them in my ear: *You will feel different when you are older and you meet someone special. When that day comes, all the negative thoughts you have about marriage will vanish in a flash, and it won't seem such a bad idea.*

She was right, but then Momma was always right. When I told Leku yes, throwing my arms around his narrow shoulders, I thought of what Momma would say if she could have been there: *I told you so, Jama*, with a big smile on her face.

Leku's uncle had trained him in the jewelry business, and he would now move to Nairobi to run the operation.

I didn't want to leave the Trust, but Leku couldn't move in there with me so I had no choice. When that bittersweet day came, I tried to be as brave as Mbegu.

Leku and I moved into a little apartment above a storefront where he could sell his products. Each day, I drove to the Trust for work, and at least once a month, I took the jeep and wandered around Nairobi National Park looking for Mbegu.

As the years went by, I never saw her, but I also never gave up hope. I always kept an eye out wherever I was, especially since occasionally a wild herd would find their way back to the Trust, sometimes with some of our former orphans in tow.

I was feeding a new arrival named Celeste on one of these occasions. She had been brought in two weeks earlier after being found abandoned in the jungle, starving to death. She was emaciated, more bone than flesh. We assumed her parents had been killed by poachers. Given her malnourished condition, she had to be fed around the clock, and I was just finishing with her third bottle of the day when I heard the rumbling of heavy footsteps in the distance and felt the ground beneath my feet vibrate.

With one hand on Celeste to keep her calm, I shielded my eyes from the sun and squinted into the horizon. I made out three elephants, the largest one leading the way while the other two followed diagonally behind, making a V shape.

As they got closer, I could see the two trailing elephants were calves, and the one in the middle had to be their mother.

"No," I gasped when I saw the mother's face. "It can't be."

I jumped to my feet to get a better look, but I didn't need to. One look at the swaggering gait and big, compassionate eyes and I knew it was her. It wasn't a mirage, it was real. There she was...my Mbegu.

She was a mother now, and she'd brought her babies to meet me.

My heart swelled so much and so fast it felt too big for my chest, as though it was going to burst right out. I secured Celeste as fast as I could, then clambered over the fence and ran toward them.

When she saw me, Mbegu started trotting. Her babies followed suit, and then she was right in front of me. I reached out to hug her, something I thought I would never get to do again. But she was so grown the closest thing to a hug that I could give her was to throw my outstretched arms against her sturdy, majestic chest. She wrapped her trunk around my shoulders and touched her snout to my cheek.

"I didn't think I'd ever see you again," I said.

She bellowed lightly in response.

Mbegu's babies flanked on either side. She nudged them toward me, making an introduction. They were shy at first, but when I hugged them and rubbed their trunks between my hands, they snuggled up to me and licked my face playfully.

"Come on," I said to Mbegu, knowing she would understand my body language. "Let's go say hi to everyone."

She followed me dutifully with her babies in tow. They looked just like she did when she was brand new to the world, wide-eyed and curious with oversized ears.

"Dafina!" I called out.

Dafina's jaw dropped. She hurried to the bell and rang it loudly. Then she ran to the gate to let us in. The staff flocked over to us from their various tasks to find out what had happened.

I watched their faces change from alarmed to incredulous to ecstatic in a few quick seconds.

"Well, look who it is!" Nathan exclaimed. "I told you she'd be back!"

"I'll be damned," said Matthew. "You are one amazing elephant, Mbegu."

"She brought her babies!" I told them proudly, as if they were mine.

We all stood, crowded together, beaming at this reunion. I stared into Mbegu's eyes just as I had done when she was young, convinced we shared a secret language. *I knew you'd be back,* I told her. *I knew I would see you again.*

"She's a big, thriving tree now," Dafina said to me, quiet enough so that only I could hear.

"What do you mean?" I asked.

"Well, you named her Mbegu because you wanted this seed to grow. And thanks to you…" Dafina opened her arms out to Mbegu as if presenting her to me. "She's all grown up."

It was true; she was a good three thousand pounds now, tall, regal, and sturdy as a baobab tree, and she had two babies of her own.

But no matter what, she would always be my little seed, my Mbegu.

GLOSSARY

Adumu   A dance performed at the coming-of-age ceremony of Maasai males.

ameaga   Is dead.

Binti   Daughter.

boma   An enclosure or fence, usually
                         made of sharp thorns, to
                         protect homes and people from
                         wild animals.

emanyatta   A group of manyattas where
                         young Maasai men (warriors)
                         stay together as part of their
                         initiation rituals.

Enkai   God.

**Enkai
tadamuiyook**   God have mercy.

enkajijik   Round huts made of mud,
                         sticks, and grass.

Eunoto   Celebration of rites of passage
                         for Maasai males.

Habu tuende   Let's go.

Iwee   You.

Kisasi	Revenge.
Kokoo	Elder.
Malaika	Angel. Title of popular Swahili love song.
manyatta	A compound of one or more homes, usually shared by families.
Mtoto wangu	My child.
shuka	Cloth worn tied around the body like a cloak by the Maasai.
ugali	Maize meal cooked into a stiff porridge.

AUTHORS' NOTE

Humans and elephants have coexisted for thousands of years, often in harmony, with both species keeping to their natural habitats and territories. However, expansion of the human population has led to our encroaching more and more on the elephants' territories. This shift has created an increasingly tense relationship between us, as both species fight for their space and survival. The current, dire reality is that people are threatening elephants' very existence. Poachers hunt elephants to profit from their tusks; some people hunt elephants for sport; and corporations and communities displace them by taking over their roaming grounds. While many people around the world have tremendous compassion for the majestic animals, their numbers continue to fall.

This novel is a work of fiction, inspired by the real threat to elephants in many countries across Africa and Asia. While we strove to faithfully depict the daily life of a Maasai girl living in a multicultural community in Kenya, we did take some liberties for the sake of the story. For example, Jama would use the metric system and therefore think in kilograms and liters rather than the pounds and gallons depicted in the book. There is of course much nuance in the life of a young Maasai girl, and we focused on showing Jama's journey from a sometimes insecure girl who dreams of having the same freedom and power as boys to an accomplished young woman who has found success, independence, and happiness.

Over the course of the story, Jama and Leku face the traumas of loss and abuse. These are serious issues, and if you or someone you know is struggling with grief or is being abused, you can seek out a trusted adult or an organization like the National Alliance for Children's Grief (childrengrieve.org) or Childhelp (childhelp.org).

We hope that you come away from Jama and

Mbegu's story with more knowledge about elephants and a better understanding as to how humans and elephants could coexist as friends rather than foes. Wouldn't that be a better world?

We take this opportunity to thank everyone who contributed to getting this book published, with special thanks to Christine Pride for her editorial assistance and Dr. Damaris Parsitau for her careful read and insight into Maasai culture. Sophia also sends thanks to Melissa de la Cruz and to everyone who has helped her in this journey of life and this project dearest to her heart.

There are elephant sanctuaries and rehabilitation centers around the world that help orphaned, injured, and other vulnerable elephants. It takes a lot to care for elephants; hence, these organizations are often looking for donations and volunteers to help in their work, which is the best way to help these majestic animals. Let us work together to provide a safe world for all its inhabitants.

ABOUT THE AUTHORS

For his prodigious imagination and championship of literacy in America, **James Patterson** was awarded the 2019 National Humanities Medal, and he has also received the Literarian Award for Outstanding Service to the American Literary Community from the National Book Foundation. He holds the Guinness World Record for the most #1 *New York Times* bestsellers, including *Max Einstein, Middle School, I Funny,* and *Jacky Ha-Ha,* and his books have sold more than 400 million copies worldwide. A tireless champion of the power of books and reading, Patterson created a children's book imprint, JIMMY Patterson, whose mission is simple: "We want every kid who finishes a JIMMY book to say, 'PLEASE GIVE ME ANOTHER BOOK.'" He has donated more than three million books to students and soldiers and funds more than four hundred Teacher and Writer Education Scholarships at twenty-one colleges and universities. He also supports forty thousand school libraries and has donated millions of dollars to independent bookstores. Patterson invests proceeds from the sales of JIMMY Patterson Books in pro-reading initiatives.

▲▼▲

Ellen Banda-Aaku is a UK-born Zambian writer who writes mainly for children. She has won several literary awards, including the Macmillan Writer's Prize for Africa, the Penguin Prize for African Writing for her novel *Patchwork*, and the Commonwealth Short Story Prize. Ellen's work—in books, radio dramas, and an award-winning documentary film—focuses on social issues impacting girls and women.

Ellen has an MA in Creative Writing from the University of Cape Town. She has lived and worked in

Zambia, South Africa, Ghana, and the UK, and currently divides her time between the UK and Zambia.

▲▼▲

Sophia Krevoy is passionate about elephant conservation. Originally from Santa Monica, California, she now lives and works in New York City.

JIMMY PATTERSON BOOKS FOR YOUNG READERS
BY JAMES PATTERSON

ALI CROSS
Ali Cross
Ali Cross: Like Father, Like Son
Ali Cross: The Secret Detective

DANIEL X
The Dangerous Days of Daniel X
Daniel X: Watch the Skies
Daniel X: Demons and Druids
Daniel X: Game Over
Daniel X: Armageddon
Daniel X: Lights Out

DOG DIARIES
Dog Diaries
Dog Diaries: Happy Howlidays
Dog Diaries: Mission Impawsible
Dog Diaries: Curse of the Mystery Mutt
Dog Diaries: Ruffing It
Dog Diaries: Dinosaur Disaster

HOUSE OF ROBOTS
House of Robots
House of Robots: Robots Go Wild!
House of Robots: Robot Revolution

I FUNNY
I Funny
I Even Funnier
I Totally Funniest
I Funny TV
I Funny: School of Laughs
The Nerdiest, Wimpiest, Dorkiest I Funny Ever

JACKY HA-HA
Jacky Ha-Ha
Jacky Ha-Ha: My Life Is a Joke
Jacky Ha-Ha: A Graphic Novel
Jacky Ha-Ha: My Life Is a Joke (A Graphic Novel)
Jacky Ha-Ha Gets the Last Laugh

KATT VS. DOGG
Katt vs. Dogg
Katt Loves Dogg

For exclusives, trailers, and other information, visit Kids.JamesPatterson.com.